RED ___ ING RYKER

The Boys of Fury

KELLY COLLINS

Copyright © 2017 by Kelly Collins

No part of this publication may be reproduced, distributed, or transmitted in any form or by any means, including photocopying, recording, or other electronic or mechanical methods, without the prior written permission of the publisher, except as permitted by U.S. copyright law. For permission requests, contact kelly@authorkellycollins.com.

The story, all names, characters, and incidents portrayed in this production are fictitious. No identification with actual persons (living or deceased), places, buildings, and products is intended or should be inferred. All products or brand names are trademarks of their respective owners.

Chapter 1

RYKER - TWENTY YEARS AGO

Raptor Savage didn't put up with losers. He didn't put up with laziness, and he didn't put up with liars. Today, I was all three.

The sunbaked asphalt pulled at my sneakers. The trees whispered, *'Turn around, run for your life.'* Each inchworm step I took closer to home slapped my backpack against my butt, but that was nothing compared to the ass-whoopin' I'd get from Dad today.

My report on Abraham Lincoln had been due today, the same report I'd told my mom I'd finished, which meant I was a liar. I hadn't done the stupid report. Hiding out in the shop and listening to the War Birds talk strategy was more fun than writing about a dead president. That made me a lazy loser. I'd gotten a big, fat zero for my grade.

Dad would shout, *The report is important, school and getting educated is the only job you have.* And I'd roll my eyes or shake my head or let my shoulders slump. Abraham Lincoln couldn't teach me a thing. He was dead.

Ask me to write about the gun that killed him, and I would have brought home an easy A. Guns, I knew.

I snaked through the bikes lined up like dominoes in the gravel parking lot as my backpack slipped from my shoulders.

So many bikes at the club meant trouble. Dad was busy, so maybe I wouldn't get a butt blistering after all.

As the president of the War Birds MC, this was Dad's world, and Mom said he ran it like he was God.

God made the laws. He made the rules. He handed down the punishments. Raptor Savage could make people shake in their sneakers with the lift of an eyebrow. I got that look a lot.

Mom always said my spirited nature would serve me well when I grew up and took over the club. Dad always put an "if" before that statement. "If he grows up."

I stepped back from the door and slipped around the side of the building. Mom was out back with my brothers, Silas and Decker. Next to them was that pesky little girl, Sparrow. She always looked up at me like I was a movie star.

"Glad you're home, sweetie." Mom never called me sweetie in front of anyone else, because that would make me seem like a sissy, but I liked when she said it. "Today's Dad's big meeting, so I need you to hang out here with the kids. I have to get inside and serve beer."

I looked around the parking lot at the motorcycles I didn't recognize. "Who's here?"

"Friends of your father's. It has nothing to do with you."

I glared at the kids playing in the dirt. "That's not true." My voice didn't sound like eight-year-old me. It sounded more like six-year-old Silas when Mom told him to take a bath. "I have to babysit, and that means it has everything to do with me." I hated babysitting. Silas was fine. At six, he took care of himself. But Decker was just a baby, which meant diapers, and then there was Sparrow. She stuck to me like gum on a shoe.

I threw my backpack toward the stairs. It skidded across the gravel and clunked to a stop against the bottom step. "Is this about Goose?" Goose was a War Bird who'd been killed last week after a cop stopped him for speeding. I didn't understand it—Goose was a good guy.

Mom looked over her shoulder toward the club entrance. "Not now, Ryker."

Uh oh. She'd called me Ryker, which meant she was losing her patience. I looked toward the kids and let out a long breath. "Okay, but is this about the cop who shot Goose?" Officer Stuart had said Goose pulled a gun first, but that had to be a big, fat lie. Goose would never shoot the police. Dad's words replayed through my head: *'That cop has been targeting motorcycle gangs. His goal is to clean up Fury.'* Fury was a small dot in the mountains. The entire town couldn't fill up the high school sports stadium. How much cleaning up did we need?

"Dad invited the Rebels over to discuss the growing tension in the area. He needs to get it under control before more people get hurt. I need you to help me out." Mom put her fingers under my chin and closed my open mouth. "Take good care of them." She didn't wait but walked into the club. The club that would someday be mine.

"Hi, Hawk." Using my nickname, Sparrow pulled on my hand. Her fingers were pink and sticky. "Want some candy?" She reached into the pocket of her dress and pulled out a piece of lint-covered licorice.

"Gross." I yanked the candy from her little fist and tossed it toward the parking lot. "It's dirty."

"It's mine." She took off toward the candy that lay in the dirt.

With two giant steps, I grabbed her around her waist, swiping her off the ground.

The rumble of motorcycle engines stopped me like I'd walked into a brick wall. Pulling in front of the club were at least ten more Rebels. "Too many."

I raced back to the playpen where Decker slept. Silas drew in the dirt with a stick, and I dropped Sparrow to her sandaled feet.

"Silas, watch them for a minute." I'd never seen the Rebels up close, and I didn't want to miss my chance.

He looked up at me with Dad's eyes. Steel, gray eyes that said it all even before the words came out. "You're supposed to stay with us."

Sparrow stomped her little feet, causing the soles of her shoes to light up. "Yeah." She looked up at me with the crazy cool eyes only she had. "You're supposed to sit with me." Her one blue and one brown eye begged me to stay.

"I'll be right back. Stay here." I crept to the corner of the club and wiggled the loose board enough to slip inside the storage room. The place smelled like leather and sweat and anger, but I tiptoed forward and slid behind the stack of crates. I pressed my ear to the crack between the boxes.

Dad's voice was loud and clear and calm. He talked about rival gangs, feuds, the sheriff, and what they were going to do.

I peeked over the crate of brake pads and counted the heads I didn't recognize. There were twenty-five Rebels in our nest. This was epic. Never had there been so many enemies in one place without someone needing a doctor.

Something creaked behind me, and I swung around.

Sparrow squeezed through the hole. *Little brat.* "What are you doing?" I whispered. "Go back," I gritted my teeth.

"No." She said, a little too loud.

I slapped my hand over her mouth. "Shh. This is a secret." I pulled her close. "You can stay if you can be quiet."

She nodded, and I went back to my hiding place. She tucked up next to me, and we listened. Or, really, I listened while she peeled the stickers from the boxes in front of us. At least she was being quiet.

All the War Birds were there. All but Goose. Kite, Dad's vice president, screamed about being targeted. Some of the members paced the room. They reminded me of the time I cornered a stray cat in the garage. Its hair stood on its back while its tail twitched from side to side.

I'd once heard someone say, '*The tension was so thick, you could cut it with a knife.*' I never understood what that meant until now. The air was thick like Mom's pudding, and it was hard to breathe.

"Your problems aren't my problems." The rebel leader leaned back and crossed his hulk-sized arms over his chest.

"It won't be long before it spreads to your club." Dad leaned forward with his elbows on his knees. "Can't we have a truce between the two clubs until the problem with the police is under control? We don't need to be fighting wars from every side."

Mom crossed in front of me with a full tray of bottled beer. I ducked lower so she wouldn't see me. Sparrow's mom, Finch, followed behind, picking up the empties. I didn't know her real name. No one went by their real name at the club. We were War Birds with names like Hawk, Raptor, Kite, and Vulture. The women always chose stupid sissy birds like Warble, Robin, or Sparrow. I looked down at the little bird next to me. She wasn't so bad. She was like me—spirited.

The front door burst open, and a pair of cops filled the doorway.

Dad jumped from his seat. "This is a private meeting," he pointed to the door, "and private property."

The big cop, the ugly one, put his hand on the butt of his gun. "Just here to keep the peace." There was something creepy about his voice. Something dangerous about the way his fingers scratched against the gun.

"Only peace here." Dad spread his arms wide enough to stretch open his leather jacket and show off his War Bird belt buckle. The belt usually held his gun, but he carried no gun today. He was in a room of enemies—unprotected. Or so it seemed. I knew Dad, and he no doubt had a plan.

Mom popped the tops off two beers and handed them to the cops.

To my surprise, they took them. I guess they didn't have to obey the rules. They were cops.

Finch passed in front of us, and Sparrow sprang to her feet. I knew she would bolt toward her mother, so I picked her up and tossed her backward toward the broken panel. She stumbled against one box, knocking it down. The loud bang shattered the silence.

Everything changed in an instant. Guns drew and shots fired—lots of shots. Bullets flew through the air with the hiss of a mosquito, only a thousand times louder. Metal hit metal with the ding of a pinball machine. Wood splintered from the rafters above.

People fell to the ground in front of me. Sparrow screamed, and I grabbed her, crouching with her behind the brake boxes, and prayed we wouldn't be next. Prayed until my mom crumpled to the ground. "Mom." Still holding Sparrow, I sprung from my hiding place and ran to where she lay in a pool of blood.

"Where are your brothers?" Her words, no more than a whisper, were hard to hear with the popping sounds filling the air. I crushed Sparrow beneath me and hugged the cement floor.

"Outside. They're safe outside." I reached for Mom, trying to find her wound.

Sparrow popped her head from under me and screamed.

Mom's eyes grew wide. "Get her out. Save her. Save your brothers." Her words slipped slow and wet from her lips. "Promise."

The wooden beams splintered, sending chunks of wood flying through the air. Clouds of white chalk burst from the walls.

My heart exploded in my chest, and tears ran down my cheeks. "Mommy."

Her head fell to the side.

"Mommy." I was a man but cried like a child. "Don't leave me." I turned her face toward mine and wiped the blood that trickled from her mouth. "I promise."

Her once bright blue eyes faded to the color of cold, gray concrete.

Bullets buzzed. People collapsed. Sparrow screamed and screamed and screamed.

I swept her into my arms and ran toward the door, but hot fire shot through my shoulder. I stumbled. I fell. Blood covered the walls, the floor, the bodies.

I scrambled to stand, but my sneakers slid on the smooth concrete. I slipped and fell over and over again until I couldn't move. I couldn't breathe. I was going to die.

Sparrow lay beside me, but she was quiet. Dead quiet. Blood seeped across her yellow dress like spilled ink on paper. The bright sunflower pattern disappeared in the crimson pool.

I'd failed. I'd failed Sparrow. I'd failed my brothers. I'd failed to keep my mom's final wish. "I promise I'll never fail anyone again," I cried. Everything turned to black.

Chapter 2

ANA-PRESENT DAY

I walked into The Wayfair Lounge, tugging at my clothes. This wasn't the place a girl went dressed in jeans and a ratty sweater, but I didn't care. I wasn't looking to hook up. I was looking for Grace.

Men in suits walked the edge of the bar, shopping the seated women like they were goods on a shelf. Waving like a lunatic in need of a white buckled jacket, Grace jumped from the corner booth. Her stilettos clicked on the wood floor, the gauzy fabric of her skirt swished around her legs.

Every man's gaze fell on those long limbs.

"You made it." She noosed my neck and pulled me in for a hug. "What do you want to drink?"

"Water." I slid into the booth and plopped my purse on top of the table.

"You can't drink water." Grace waved to the bartender, motioned to her Cosmo, and held up two fingers.

"I can't afford anything but water." I pulled my wallet from my purse and opened it to reveal a lone ten-dollar bill. It was the only money I had until next week when I'd get paid for my last design job

—a flier for the new donut shop on Colfax. It wasn't the work I'd envisioned when I graduated with a graphics design degree, but it paid some of the bills.

"This one is on me." She looked me up and down, then frowned. "If you had dressed for the place, the drinks could have been on him." She nodded toward Mr. Pinstripe, leaning against the wall and staring. Staring at Grace. I might as well have been invisible.

I grabbed Grace's glass, and the drink sloshed over the side. I sucked the sticky liquid that ran down my fingers.

"Keep doing that, and the whole bar will buy you drinks. It won't matter what you're wearing."

I popped my finger from my mouth. Yep, at least a dozen men zoned in on my mouth—my lips—my tongue. The heat of a blush rose to my cheeks.

The bartender set a tray of drinks on our table. He looked around the room and nodded toward several men. "Compliments of your admirers."

Grace pulled out a twenty and slid it in the bartender's pocket. "Thanks, Tony."

"No problem. Cosmos for the next round?" he asked as if we'd slammed the first round.

I shook my head. "No more for me." After two of these, I'd be done. Three would have me slurring my words. Four, and I'd be waking up someplace strange with a hairy chest pressed against my face.

"Keep them coming, and keep them the same." Grace gave him her Hollywood smile. "No one wants a sick date. You know the saying: Mix your liquor, never been sicker." She toasted her martini at the crowd. "Here's to man-whore Mondays."

The bartender laughed and left.

"I've got to stop coming here with you." It was the truth. The past several Mondays, I'd tipped back a few too many martinis and made too many poor choices. Mondays never produced the right kind of men. I wanted more than an in-the-minute Mike. I wanted a long-term Luke. "I don't get it. I'm smart. I'm funny. I'm low maintenance. I'm not crazy. I can pull off sexy. Shouldn't I be beating men off with a stick?"

"With a stick?" Grace was half a martini to full-on giddy drunk. "In my experience, they'd prefer you beat them off with your hand." She made an obscene gesture. "I think that might be your problem."

I grabbed her hand and pushed it to the table, making her wobble on her heels. "Sit down before you fall down. How many of these have you had?"

She held up her hand and raised one finger, then snapped it to two. She looked at her drink, the one I'd drunk half of, and bent her second finger down. Grace was well on her way to a terrible Tuesday of regret.

"I read an article this week that said orphans have trouble finding a significant other when they grow up." She shrugged in a noncommittal way that meant, *I don't know if it's true or not.*

"Lucky for me, I have Grams." I'd been living with her since the day my parents died in a car crash. I rubbed the area on my shoulder where the rebar had lodged. It still ached sometimes, especially when the weather was cold. A constant reminder of a day I couldn't remember. When I closed my eyes, the canvas of my early life was always fuzzy. I heard the screams. I smelled the smoke. I felt my heart race and plummet to a stop. Then, nothing.

I jumped in my seat when my phone rang. The screen lit up while the "Imperial Death March" played.

"Are you going to answer?" Grace picked up my phone and laughed. "Who's Vulture?"

Air rushed out of my mouth in a huff. "Landlord."

She looked down at her phone. "It's the fifth. Didn't you pay your rent?"

I pretended to pound my head against the table. The nearly empty martini glasses shook and jingled.

"Paid what I could."

"Which was?" She raised her hand to Tony again. "Talk of finances requires liquid reinforcement."

"Not enough." I drank martini number two just before Tony brought number three. "I don't want to talk about it." I was down to a blowup mattress and a lawn chair. The only thing I hadn't sold was my computer and my phone—both requirements for work.

"Okay. So, what do you want to talk about?"

I needed to have some fun. "Let's talk about my next date." I looked over the rim of my glass around the bar. People were pairing up now. All it took were a few drinks and a two on the sexy scale to turn into a ten.

Grace scooted around the booth until her back faced the wall. Her green eyes swept the room like laser-guided missiles. "What about him?" She nodded toward the door, where three corporate America men stood sipping dark beer.

"Which one?"

"Mr. Tall, Dark, and Dapper." She rimmed her glass with her finger until it sang something akin to a B flat.

I looked at the darkest-haired man in the group. He was fine if you liked trust fund-babies and country clubs. My tastes were less refined. "He's such a peacock." I preferred a man who demanded respect with a single look while wearing jeans and a T-shirt.

"It's always the birds with you." She leaned over the table as if her sight were failing. After three drinks, maybe it was. "He's more of a rooster, don't you think? I love a rooster's cocksure demeanor—the way they strut their stuff."

"What you like is their cock-a-doodle-doo."

Grace burst out a laugh. "That, among other things." She licked the sugared rim of her glass, and I was certain any man looking had gone weak in the knees.

"What other things?" I barely refrained from rolling my eyes. Grace and I had been inseparable since the day I showed up at St.

Mary's dressed in my plaid uniform and new light-up sneakers. *Sisters from different misters*, but with totally different outlooks.

"I don't know. Handsome in that I've-got-a-Maserati way. And look at his friend."

One guy had a beak for a nose; the other, a barrel for a belly. "Which one? The toucan, or the grouse?"

"I like a man with a strong nose." She looked around the bar again. "Okay, tell me which of these guys is the bird for your nest."

I giggled to myself, because anyone coming to my nest would have to embrace simple living and ramen noodles. My eyes went from man to man until I'd rounded the room. "If men were birds, and I had to choose one, it wouldn't be anyone here."

"Oh, come on." She pinched my arm. She had a way of getting the tiniest bit of skin—enough to send a pulse of pain through every nerve ending. "Play with me."

"I'm serious." I looked at all the pretty boys dressed in Brooks Brothers. "All these guys are birds of paradise. They stand around and look pretty." I drank the rest of my martini. "They don't know what they want. They come here and peck at the feed every night…I want the guy who's not afraid to swoop down and fight for me."

"You're asking for a bird of prey." She bit her lip and raised her brow. "You know they eat everything in their path?"

"Being eaten doesn't sound half bad." I picked up my purse and slid out of the booth. "I'll leave you to your peacocks and roosters. I'll wait for my hawk."

Chapter 3

ANA

After three sleepless nights, I walked into Coohills, and the smell of fresh-baked bread filled my senses. I closed my eyes and breathed in the calming scent. The last time Grams baked was three years ago, before dementia set in.

I should have known something was wrong when she used salt instead of sugar. The worst chocolate chip cookies I'd ever eaten, but I choked down a few because she'd made them special for me.

My eyes adjusted to the low lights of the restaurant. Fresh flowers and lit candles sat on top of linen-covered tables. This place was a mile above the soup kitchen I'd eaten at last night. Here the people dressed better and spoke in full sentences. I'd even bet the hundred bucks I'd borrowed from Grace that they showered with regularity.

"Welcome to Coohills." The host stepped up to the host station. Dressed in black slacks, a white shirt, his outfit matched mine.

Perfect, I was dressed like the help except for the red tie all the servers wore. I was underdressed to be a waiter, overdressed for my normal life and did not understand how to dress for this meeting.

"I have a reservation under the name Ana Barrett." I shifted back and forth in the black patent leather pumps that I only wore to job interviews and funerals. "I requested a quiet table." I gripped my computer case and followed the man to the back corner of the restaurant.

"Will this do?" He pulled out a chair for me, and I sat.

"Perfect. Thank you." I ordered a diet soda. With shaking fingers, I pulled several sample brochures from a folder and fanned them out on the table.

Thank God for Grace's peacocks. She'd sent the smooth-talking Dexter Weston to me. If he liked my work, At Flight Graphics might take off, and then I'd be able to splurge on a few grocery items. Milk and butter for my morning oatmeal sounded decadent —sinful, even.

I'd been trying to spread my wings since graduation. Grams had helped as much as she could, but she'd never had much in the way of money, and now that she required long-term home care, she had nothing. Every penny of her Social Security check and Gramps's small pension went toward her rent and at-home nurse.

I ran my fingers over the projects I'd picked up over the years. "Wish me luck." I tapped the bird I'd hidden in each one. One was a shadow of a blue jay in the clouds. I'd placed a pigeon in a tree of a recycling company brochure. I'd even turned a piece of cotton candy into a bird for a child's birthday invitation. Birds made me feel safe.

I sipped at my soda and waited and waited and waited. I checked my phone for the third time. I'd been five minutes early, he was five late. Lunchtime traffic?

I readjusted the samples and put them in order according to basic color theory—red, orange, yellow, green, blue, purple. I looked at my phone. Ten minutes. I swallowed the lump building in my throat.

My phone rang and showed an unknown number. "Thank God." I was sure Dexter was calling to say he was running late.

"Hello, this is Ana," I said in my happiest voice.

"Hi, Ana, this is Dexter." His voice sounded like old Mr. Greer, the mortician who'd embalmed Gramps. Sucking out the lifeblood from his clients had sucked every bit of emotion out of the man. Talking to him was like talking to cardboard, and Dexter Weston sounded the same.

"Do you need directions?"

"No. I've decided to run in another direction and can't make the meeting today."

Run in another direction? What did that mean? Was it literal? Figurative? I had no idea. "We can reschedule. How about tomorrow?"

"No, Ana." He cleared his throat. "What I mean is, I don't need your services. We will spend our money on social media this quarter, but thank you for your time."

My stomach clenched and forced burning acid to my throat. This wasn't happening. I needed work. I needed money. Hell, I needed to eat. I swallowed hard, and fire slid down to my stomach. "Dexter, social media is important, but it's only one facet of marketing." Somehow, I kept the quake out of my voice. "For a well-rounded approach, you should split your efforts between print and digital. I can prepare both for you." At this point, I'd split anything as long as I got a piece of the pie.

Silence stretched, and my heart leapt. He was thinking. I had a chance. "I can offer you a new client discount of twenty-five percent."

Muffled voices sounding like people talking underwater filled the void. I held my breath.

"Sorry, Ana, what was that you said?"

My chin touched my chest. He hadn't been thinking. He hadn't been listening. "I offered you a discount as a first-time customer." I didn't know if he could hear the resignation my voice. The disappointment of another lost job crushed my soul.

"I'm not interested."

"But—" The line went dead.

I couldn't breathe. I couldn't think. I couldn't afford the soda.

But I took a deep breath, blinked back the tears, and asked for the check.

The waiter gave me one of those looks where kindness and understanding were heaped with pity. "It's on me."

I hated the pity but appreciated the effort. "Thanks." I gathered my things and pulled a five-dollar bill out of my purse. The soda might have been on him, but I'd occupied a table that could have made him money from a paying customer.

Grams once told me to never borrow trouble, but once outside, I lifted my eyes to the sky and asked, "What now?"

I trudged home and found out why you should never question the universe. A big yellow eviction notice hung from my front door.

"AND HE DIDN'T EVEN COME to meet you?" Grace sat on my lawn chair and opened the second bottle of wine she'd brought. The first bottle had disappeared while I explained how I'd planned to dominate the world with this one client. Now it was all gone.

I slid down the wall to sit on the floor. "Nope." No meeting. No client. No hope. At Flight Graphics would never soar. "Kind of like getting a dear Jane letter, right?" I poured the wine into two red Solo cups and opened Grace's I'm-sorry Styrofoam container filled with beef and broccoli and pork fried rice.

"I can't believe I slept with that guy." She opened her container of orange chicken and white rice.

I speared a piece of broccoli and chewed off the tree-like end. "I told you not to trust the peacocks."

"Pea cock is about right. The tiniest thing I've ever seen."

"It's the little dicks that become the biggest ones in business. It's how they compensate for their shortcomings."

"You could be right. I've found that the men with the biggest egos have the smallest set of balls."

My throaty groan filled the air. "Must we talk about man parts while we're eating? This is the first meal I've had in days that didn't come freeze-dried, and I'd like to keep it down." I stuck out my tongue and faked a gagging noise.

She flung a piece of her chicken at me. It bounced off my shoulder and rolled across the hardwood floor. Her eyes took in my empty apartment. "I love what you've done with the place. You've taken minimalist decorating to new heights."

I unfolded my crossed legs and shimmied across the floor to clean it up. "It'll make moving easy."

We both looked at the yellow eviction notice sitting on my makeshift desk—a TV stand I'd found in the alleyway on garbage day.

"You know you can stay with me." Grace lived in a one-bedroom apartment on the good side of Denver. With her salary as an executive assistant, she paid her rent. Her closet was full of smart clothes. Her wine rack stocked.

"I have thirty days to vacate this castle." When I closed my eyes, I could see the camel colored sofa I wanted to put where the plastic chair sat. The cream sheers I planned for the bare windows. All dreams crushed by reality. "I'll figure it out by then."

We sat in silence, eating our meals until my phone rang. I picked it up and looked at the number. Not one I recognized, so I set it back on the floor.

Two bites later, it rang again. This time, Grace grabbed it. "Let me deal with this." We both knew it was a bill collector that I couldn't pay, and they were never nice. "Hello," she said in a don't-mess-with-me tone. Her flaming red hair was a dead giveaway of the fire and irritation that burned inside her. "Yes?" Her voice rose questioningly.

Her face went pale. "Okay." She hung up and dropped the phone to the floor. "Oh, sweetie," she said. Large, sad eyes stared back at me. "It's your grandmother."

Chapter 4

RYKER

I spent my entire morning trying to get the damn throttle unstuck. The bike purred to life around ten and sent me hurtling through the fence an hour later. Damn cable pinched and stuck when I hit thirty-five on a straightaway. Thank God I had a helmet on. I rubbed the knot in my shoulder and kicked the tire. The stupid thing was old, but special.

I couldn't get an even steady idle on the bike all day, but the rumble in my stomach had worked its way to a ravenous growl. I tossed my wrench aside and walked outside The Nest.

"You give that thing its last rites yet?" Nate kicked off the side of the truck and smacked me on the back.

A jolt of pain ripped through my shoulder. "It's coming along." I rotated my arm, trying like hell to get the kink out.

"It's dead, bro." He climbed into the driver's side of the black truck. I opened the passenger door. The diesel engine coughed to life and spit out a black cloud. "Ready to eat?"

"Ready two hours ago. I'm starving." I climbed in and buckled up. One near miss was enough for the day.

"Dude, why do you tool with that piece of shit?" He pulled out of the gravel parking lot and onto the highway.

"Some things can't ever be left behind." In the side-view mirror, the garage faded from view. It was another thing I couldn't let go.

"I get that it was your dad's, and that's kind of beautiful in a screwed-up way, but you've gotta move on. I mean, look at you." Nate slapped his hand on the steering wheel. "You're living above the site where most of your family died. Who sticks around the place where the worst day of their life happened?"

"It reminds me of who I am."

"I'll tell you who you are. You're a broke bastard with a chip the size of a continent on your shoulder. When's the last time that place turned a profit?"

I turned my head toward the window. There wasn't much to say on that subject. Nate shut his mouth and drove to the diner.

Before we'd even slid into the booth, Hanna rushed over. "Hey, Ryker." She leaned over adjusting the blinds, but there was nothing wrong with the blinds. She rubbed her chest against my shoulder, copping a feel, the waitress way.

Last week, she'd climbed into my lap while showing me the weekly specials. The same specials they'd been serving for years. I never gave in, but the damn woman never gave up.

"Burgers and fries times two." I gave her a single glance, then rearranged my silverware. There was no use leading her on when nothing would come of her walk-by boobings.

The minute Hannah left, Nate leaned across the table. "You need to hit that."

I watched her slink behind the counter and pour our iced teas. "She's not my type."

Nate laughed. "Now you have a type?"

Hannah was back in seconds with two iced teas and a smile that said I'm all yours. And she probably would have been if the cook hadn't yelled, "Order up." She grumbled all the way back to the kitchen.

I waited until she was out of earshot. "I like them here today and gone tomorrow." I opened four packets of sugar and dumped them into my tea. "Not saying I'd mind getting with Hannah. I mean, look at that ass. But I'm not capable of anything beyond a quick lay."

"I wouldn't spread the quick rumor around. That could kill your reputation."

"Maybe, but no one would call me on it. I'd kick their ass." My reputation had little to do with what hung between my legs. It had everything to do with what hung in the air around me. I was moody. I was mean. People crossed the street to avoid me. Losing my family had left my chest a cavernous hole filled with torment and regret.

"I read an article the other day about how orphans have trouble finding a significant other once they grow up."

I reached across the table and popped the little asshole across the side of the head. "Shut the hell up, Nate." I picked up my tea and drank it straight down. "I'm not talking about that day."

"Dude, calm down." He rubbed his red ear. "I'm not talking about that day either. I'm talking about a damn article that said orphaned kids struggle with relationships. That's all." He raised his hands like a shield, waiting for my next strike.

"Okay, Freud. You're so damn smart. Tell me why my heart is a hollowed-out shell."

Nate dropped his hands and his jaw. "Is it? I was thinking you had trust issues. Maybe you were afraid of letting people get close or some shit like that. I'm not qualified to talk about your shriveled-up heart."

"It's not shriveled. You can't shrivel something with no mass."

Hannah walked back and set two plates with burgers and fries on the table. "What's shriveled up?" Her eyes traveled down my body.

Nate's long bangs fall over his eyes. His lips lifted into a sarcastic smile. "Hey, Hawk, Hannah looks like she's offering to help with your little shriveling problem."

I clenched my fist to keep from smacking him again. Only my family and the War Birds called me Hawk.

"What I got can't be confused with little." I snatched a handful of fries from his plate. "And shriveled? Please. Harder than granite. Stronger than titanium." I shoved the fries in my mouth and gave Nate an I'm-going-to-kick-your-ass look.

Hannah used her hip to nudge me over and slid into the booth next to me. "I'd like to help in any way I can, Hawk. Hard, soft, shriveled, granite. I can be your girl."

I pushed my hip toward Hannah, sending her flying out of the booth and landing flat on her ass. "My name is Ryker, and you're not my girl."

She hopped to her feet and rubbed her bottom. "Not yet, you asshole, but you're lucky I like a challenge."

Nate choked on his burger. He took a drink of his tea, but his laughter made it come out his nose. "You hear what she said? She thinks you're an asshole."

Hannah picked up a wad of napkins and shoved them in Nate's face. "You're an asshole, too."

Nate smiled like she'd told him he was some kind of god. He raised his hand and high-fived me across the table. "I've graduated to asshole."

Hannah growled and stormed off.

I stared at my best friend. My only friend. "When was that attribute ever in question?"

Nate pointed at me like Uncle Sam in a recruitment poster. "I defer to the king. Now back to your shriveled heart."

I picked up a fry and flung it at him. The problem was, Nate was too quick. The damn fry sailed past him and hit old man Dickson in the head.

"Who's getting the toe of my boot?" The old man's voice boomed, and he turned around.

I bolted from my seat. "I apologize, sir—" Standing in front of Mr. Dickson was like getting called to the principal's office "—but

Nate here was talking about man-parts in front of sweet Hannah, and I thought it would shut him up. However, I overshot my intended target."

"Young man, manners are like money. You have them, and you're rich. You don't, and you're not." Mr. Dickson reached over the back of the booth and cuffed Nate upside his head. "You're poor, son, but there's hope for you yet." The old man's steely gaze didn't waver from Nate. "Get your skinny tail up from that seat and apologize to Hannah and make sure you leave her an extra tip for putting up with your sorry self."

The old man waited for Nate to leave the booth before he turned back toward his table.

I laughed myself into a stomachache.

Hannah looked past Nate to me. When our eyes met, she pulled him to her and pressed her lips to his. If I were normal, I would have felt something: anger, annoyance, the need to beat her brain to a pulp. Hell, I didn't have feelings. That wiring in my brain had shorted out. I felt nothing.

Nate jerked away. "What the hell?" He wiped his mouth like his lips had been coated in a communicable disease. He raced back to our booth.

"Maybe you should hit that," I said.

"No way, man. She wants you in the worst way." He looked over his shoulders at Satan in a white apron. "I'd be lucky to have someone want me that bad."

"You're luckier than you think." Nate's mother had been sick that awful day, so she'd stayed home. His dad had been there but survived. His family remained intact. Mine was gone.

Chapter 5

ANA

Nothing like bad news to sober me up and put life in perspective. Food and housing and bills meant nothing. Grams, Grams, Grams. I wasn't ready for her to be gone.

I gave Grace a big hug and rushed toward Grams apartment. I stood outside looking at the faded, peeling paint of the tired apartment building. This had been her home for 40 years.

Her initial forgetfulness I'd been able to blame on old age. I picked up the slack for everything that wasn't getting done. I paid the bills, did the laundry, shopped for food. We curled up on the couch every night and watched reruns of *All in the Family*, her favorite '70s sitcom.

But things got worse. Grams stopped showering. I missed a lot of school. She stopped eating. I managed to graduate. She stopped being Grams. The day she started the kitchen on fire was a sobering moment. I couldn't leave her alone but couldn't cope alone. I'd hired a home health aide and moved out to make room for the overnight nurse. That's when my life turned to shit.

I rushed up the stone-steps past the wall of mailboxes to the elevator. I tapped my foot on the worn black and white tile and pushed and pushed and pushed the button. In the corner, a potted plant of plastic flowers faded. The kind of flowers people put on graves.

"Stay with me, Grams."

The elevator doors screeched open, and I climbed in and pushed the button for floor five. The small box lurched up like my 120 pounds was pressing the weight limit. It chugged along until it came to an abrupt stop. I ran past the faded wallpaper, faded paint, faded lives lingering behind closed doors. Each step beat me up for not being here.

Things had been so hectic lately. With the missed meetings and flubbed presentations, I'd failed to get the business off the ground. Each task was a time vampire that sucked the minutes from my days. Failure became synonymous with my name. Business failures. Life failures. Failure to recognize Grams' downward spiral.

The at-home nurse had told me a stroke was only a matter of time. But it wasn't time. Grams was all I had left. She had to be okay.

I opened the door and edged forward, tiptoeing into the apartment. My heart thumped in my ears, breaking the deathly silence around me. I moved forward one step at a time to its haunting rhythm.

A soft glow came from Grams' bedroom. A ray of light spilled into the dark corridor like a beckoning beacon of doom.

Gone was the smell of Gramps' aftershave. Gone was the sugared, cinnamon aroma of my youth. Gone was the Aqua Net Hairspray Grams used to get three days out of her hairdo. The place smelled like antiseptic, plastic, and death.

I moved like molasses in winter to her bedside. She looked like a child, so weak, so frail, and so small.

The nurse rose from the bedside chair. "I'll leave you two alone." The squishing sound of her white nursing shoes faded with each step until it completely disappeared.

My knees buckled, and I collapsed to the olive shag carpet next to the bed. "Grams," I cried. I held her frail hand. My tears followed the veiny path of her crepe-like skin. "I'm sorry I wasn't here all week." I swiped at my tears and looked at the beautiful woman lying in front of me. I pushed back the shock of white hair that lay across her forehead. It was as soft and white and wispy as the clouds. She looked peaceful in her sleep.

The room was warm, but a bone-chilling shudder shook me. I adjusted the collar of her pink flannel pajamas and pulled the quilt up under her chin.

Pull it together. My shoulders unfurled with each deep breath I took. "I have a job," I lied. I wanted to fill her head with positive thoughts. "It's such a good job, Grams. At Flight Graphics is taking off."

With the edge of the sheet, I wiped the drool from the corner of her mouth. "I got a new chair for my apartment." The smile on my face was fake. I'd once heard that if you smiled while you spoke, it showed up in your words. I wanted my words to sound cheerful. I would never tell Grams I'd found the lawn chair on the curb on trash day. She'd be appalled at how I lived.

"Get better so we can make cookies and drink tea together."

Grams' eyes fluttered and opened. Her weathered hand pointed to the painting on the wall across from the foot of the bed.

"That's the picture I gave you two years ago for Christmas." Art pumped through my veins. No day was complete without a doodle, a dabble of paint, or a dash of artistic inspiration. I'd been drawing, painting, creating ever since I could remember breathing.

Her fingers shook, but she pointed to the painting like she wanted to see it up close.

"You want to see it?"

I forced myself away from Grams and to the picture of a small brown bird that sat alone on a leafless branch. I lifted the painting from the wall. Although I'd painted the bird alone, I'd always thought the picture hopeful. I carried it back to the woman who'd raised me.

A tear slipped from her eye.

Seated on the edge of her bed, I held the picture at eye level.

Her lips moved, but nothing recognizable came from her mouth. The stroke had stolen her words. She stabbed her gnarled finger at the bird painted in the corner of the canvas and then poked the scar on my shoulder like a crow pecking at roadkill.

I didn't know what she was thinking—or even whether she *was* thinking—but she seemed adamant about something. Her lips twitched into something like a smile, and her eyes closed. Her hand fell to my lap. She was gone. Not gone to sleep, but gone for good.

AFTER THE PRIEST said a few words, I sat in the front pew of the church with Grace. The saint statues around the room looked down on me in unneeded judgment. I'd judged myself. I'd promised to be there, not only at the end, but all the in-between times. I had failed.

The sanctuary was silent, as if the whole world had stopped for a moment to say goodbye to Agatha Barrett.

"She's better off," Grace whispered.

I snagged a Kleenex from the box that sat next to me. People always said stuff like that. Shit like *she's no longer suffering*, or *she's in a better place*, but how did they know? I sniffled.

This was the second time I could remember sitting in this church saying goodbye to someone I loved. I'd been here once before, for Gramps' funeral ten years ago, but I had no memory of burying my parents. I had no recollections of anything before coming to live with my grandparents.

An elderly woman I recognized as one of Grams' neighbors shuffled toward me with her walker and patted my hand as she passed. A few people came and went, but the turnout had been small. Grams kept to herself. The first part of her life had been all about Gramps. The last twenty years had been all about me.

Her home health care aides stopped by my side one by one.

They gave me words of encouragement. Her attorney swung by to remind me of our get-together that afternoon at the apartment.

The funeral director approached. "It's time to take her to the cemetery." He apologized for rushing us, but there was another service starting soon.

I glanced back to the double doors of the church, where another casket waited. I gathered my things and followed Grams' casket out the side door.

At the grave, the sun still shone. The birds still sang. Life went on for everyone but Agatha Barrett. Grace held my hand, and the dark brown soil swallowed Grams.

"Goodbye." I placed the wreath of flowers Grace had bought over the mound of dirt and walked away.

"You okay?" Grace wound her arm through mine and walked me to her car.

"No. The other day you called me an orphan, and I snapped at you. Now I *am* an orphan. I have nobody."

Grace pulled me to her side and wrapped her arm around my shoulders. "You have me."

I buried my head against her shoulder and followed her to the car. The sun released its warmth around me, but I was cold and empty inside.

We arrived back at the small apartment. It was odd walking into the place knowing she was gone. The room was void of hospital supplies. Void of the antiseptic smell. Void of life.

I stood in the middle and waited for Grams to holler at me to come give her some sugar. I always threw myself into her arms and gave her a kiss. When I was a kid, I'd come home from school and find her in the kitchen, waiting with cookies and tea. Those days were long gone, but the memories would be mine forever.

"Are you sure you don't want me to stay until the attorney gets here?" Grace looked between the door and me.

I knew she'd stay if I asked, but I wouldn't ask. Grace had already missed several days helping with the arrangements.

I walked around the room and traced the dusty knickknacks with my fingers. "No, I'm going to pack up her things. The landlord stopped by yesterday and told me he had someone moving in the first of the month."

"You can't catch a break, can you? That's two places you have to vacate before the month is up."

One look around the apartment, and I knew there wasn't much here worth saving.

"My place is easy. I only have to toss out a lawn chair and a TV tray. The rest I'll shove into the back of my car." Thank goodness I'd gotten Gramps' old Jeep when he passed. Grams had never learned how to drive, and given that my parents had died in that horrific car crash, who could blame her?

"I'm a phone call away. Let's meet for dinner tomorrow at Luigi's at six—my treat. You can tell me all about the millions Grams had stashed away that we didn't know about." Only Grace could make me smile at a time like this.

I hugged her tight, like she might disappear forever. "See you tomorrow." It was hard letting her go, but it was necessary. I couldn't pull Grace into the dark abyss with me. She was light like the sun, as warm as its rays, and right now I was cold and dark.

The apartment was old and dated like the seventy-two-year-old woman who had lived here. She'd collected clowns, which I'd always found kind of creepy. I rummaged through the curio cabinet and found the happiest-looking one of the bunch. It would be the only one I'd keep. Next, I walked to her bedroom. Being Catholic, she had the obligatory crucifix hanging on the wall and a statue of Mary next to her bed. I picked up her family Bible and set it aside to pack. The only art that ever hung from the light blue walls was the painting I'd given her. I'd keep that, too.

It took an hour to box up her clothes for the homeless shelter. The woman in charge promised to pick them up later if I left them in the lobby.

The door buzzer rang as I organized the kitchen. I pressed the intercom. "Hello?"

"Ana? This is Taylor Goodwin. Can I come up?" He spoke with authority, the kind of voice found in the courtroom, and I wondered whether he'd always been a probate attorney.

"I'm in 5G." I pressed the buzzer. I wanted to slap myself, because he knew where Grams lived. He would have visited her at least once before to draw up her will.

The cogs and pulleys of the old elevator creaked and croaked until it made its way up to the fifth floor, where I waited. The doors opened up and spit out a ball of a man. He was well-fed and well-dressed.

"Ana?" He held out the doughy hand that wasn't gripping his briefcase and led me to the kitchen.

Yep, the man had been here. The kitchen was the only place Grams entertained.

"Tea?" I opened the cupboard and pulled out a clown mug, mocking the somber situation with its brilliant red smile.

"No, thank you." Mr. Goodwin remained standing. "This shouldn't take long."

I closed the door on the laughing clown's face.

"What can I do for you?" I pulled out my usual chair and sat.

"As you know, your grandmother didn't have much in the way of liquid assets." He looked around the kitchen, as if making a point. "She had one thing she wanted you to have besides her small life insurance policy." He reached into his briefcase and pulled out several papers and something shiny he palmed in his pudgy fist.

"She left me life insurance?" I had no idea there would be anything of financial value, certainly not an insurance policy.

"Don't get too excited. It's a small five-thousand-dollar policy."

I gripped the table.

"Are you okay?"

"I'm shocked. I expected nothing."

Mr. Goodwin shrugged as if her gift was unimportant, when in reality it was the most generous thing I could have received. Five thousand dollars meant I could eat, put gas in my car, and find another place to live.

He placed a piece of paper on the table in front of me. "Sign here and here." He pointed to two sticky arrows already in place.

"Is this for the insurance?"

"No, I have the information you need to contact them. This is the deed to the house."

I shook my head to rattle some sense into his words. "What house?"

He pointed to the address at the top of the page. "Your grandmother purchased this house years ago for pennies on the dollar after the old owners died, and the taxes weren't paid."

I stared at the man as if he were a clown from Grams' collection. "If she had a house, then why would she stay in this apartment?" The place was a total shithole. Not as much of a shithole as the place I lived in, but it had been built in the '70s and never updated. Avocado appliances were still in their places on the harvest gold linoleum floor. A percolator that died years ago took up residence on the faded gold Formica counter.

"All I know is, you're the owner of a house in Fury, Colorado." He handed me a key, collected the signed deed, and walked away.

"I have a house."

The front door clicked closed.

"I have a key." I opened my palm to reveal a lone key on a ring. A key that would undoubtedly change my life.

Chapter 6

RYKER

In the passenger seat, I waited for Nate to walk out of the diner. Inside, Hannah was probably making a move on him. She wasn't a bad woman, but she wasn't my kind of woman. When Nate climbed into the driver's seat, I asked, "Did she blow you in the back room?"

"What?" He looked down at his open zipper. "Screw you. I was using the head."

"I use my head, too, when someone's sucking it." I slapped the dashboard and laughed. "Let's go. I've got shit to do."

Nate turned the key and gunned the engine. "She likes you. She's lonely. You're lonely. It's the perfect setup." Dust billowed behind us, creating a cloud.

"I'm not lonely. I'm alone—by choice. I happen to like my company more than anyone else's."

"Except mine."

"You're all right, but I'm not letting you blow me."

He pulled in front of The Nest. "Get the hell out of my truck, asshole. You need to get laid. You'd be nicer if you did."

I opened the door and walked a few feet away before I flipped him the bird. He was probably right. I'd been a bear to be around lately. I always got that way around the anniversary of my parents' death.

I didn't bother going inside. I headed straight to my car and took off.

The old house sat abandoned, the grass shin high, the flowers strangled by weeds. It had been almost a year since I'd been here, twenty since they'd died, a lifetime since I'd given a damn about anyone, especially me.

I trudged to the shed in back and pulled out the old push mower, a hoe, and a rake. I was halfway through the first flowerbed, sweaty and pissed, and took my anger out on the weeds I yanked from the ground.

"Is that you, Ryker?" Mona called from across the street. She held her hand over her eyes like a shield. The woman was nearly blind, but I swear she saw better than anyone I knew. She never missed a thing. She pointed to a drink pitcher sitting on her front porch table. "You want some lemonade?"

I pulled a dandelion from the roots. I wanted a lot of things, and none were as tame as lemonade, but I'd never turn Mona down. She'd been my teacher when everything went down, and she was the first person who visited me in the hospital as I recovered.

I rubbed at the scar on my right shoulder. It still ached at times. Mostly when the weather changed, but it ached the most on the last day of April. Every year without fail.

I dropped the hoe and walked across the street.

"How ya doing, Ms. Charming?" This was our game. I'd use some type of inappropriate word pairing, or what she'd call lazy English, and I'd get a lesson. Mona's lessons brought me as close to feeling loved as I'd been in years.

Mona still had the presence of a take-no-prisoners teacher but creaked into one of her wicker chairs. She was getting old. "Say it correctly, Ryker." Old, but definitely not soft. She handed me a glass of lemonade, and my mouth already puckered. No instant mix for her, her fresh-squeezed lemonade would put a pucker on a saint.

"How are you doing, Ms. Charming?" I enunciated each word. She didn't like slang, and she didn't put up with a lazy tongue.

"Come here, Ryker, and give this old woman a hug. And for God's sake, call me Mona; otherwise, I'll feel like a damn pedophile."

I chuckled and wrapped my arms around her, squeezing like I never wanted to let go. She'd always been there for me. She wrote letters and sent cookies when I went to jail. She sent a car to pick me up and bring me back home when I got released. Once, she'd even paid my back taxes so I didn't lose the shop. Mona wasn't blood, but she was family.

We sat in silence and sipped our drinks. Across the street, the white paint peeled, and the unkempt yard reminded me how much I'd failed. Shame consumed me.

"What do you think she'd be like now?" She asked.

I closed my eyes and thought about *her*. Never once in all these years had we discussed *her*. "I imagine she'd be gorgeous. Her mother was." Her mother was a tiny little thing everyone called Finch. Not the prettiest name, but it fit her. I closed my eyes and pictured the little girl with brown pigtails and a yellow sunflower dress. Her smile could melt my heart, and her stubbornness could test a saint.

"What a tragedy. So many lives changed that day."

"Not a day I like to dwell on."

"Here's the thing, Ryker."

I swallowed a groan. I was in for a lesson. Anytime Mona started a sentence with *Here's the thing*, there was some point she wanted to emphasize. "I'm all ears." Hell, if I didn't focus, she'd grab me by an ear and yank it until she had my full attention. I'd spent many a day with flaming red lobes.

"Pain that's not transformed is transferred." She sat back and smiled.

"Have you been listening to those Zen Buddhist tapes again?" Macular degeneration had taken Mona's sight little by little over the past ten years. As an educator, she'd loved written words, but when her sight was stolen, she'd turned to audiobooks. Lately, she'd been listening to some singing monks from Tibet.

"No, I've been thinking about that day. Thinking how you've been living with the burden since you were eight years old. Isn't it time you turned it into something else?"

I set my glass down so hard, the table shook. "How do you transform that situation into something better? Dozens of people died that day. Kids were orphaned. Women were widowed. Lives were ruined. I broke my promise."

"Oh, pish, you were eight. Cut yourself some slack. Stop being angry, and start living your life. Transform your pain. Find a girl. Fall in love. Make babies."

"I'll work on it." I hated to lie to Mona, but what purpose did it serve to beat her with the truth? I would never move past the day an entire town was slaughtered, because I couldn't follow directions.

"I wish it was July," she said with a dreamy tone.

I rose from my seat and leaned over to give her a kiss on the cheek. "July is way too hot. Why would you miss July?"

"That's the month you mow shirtless."

"I love you, Mona."

"I'm too old to have your babies."

I left her on the porch laughing like a lunatic. This yard needed more attention than I was giving it, and I shouldn't let it wither.

I beat the ground with the hoe, hacking at the weeds that had choked out the life of everything beautiful that once lived here. Once the ground was turned and tilled, I moved on to the grass. When I finished the job, I stood on the curb and stared at the house. It was still empty and lifeless, like my heart, but at least something good had happened today. I'd kept my promise to keep her memory alive by preserving her home.

She'd loved this house. This garden. She had once picked a

yellow daisy and brought it to me. "Here, Hawk." She'd pushed the bedraggled flower into my hand.

"What do you want me to do with this?" I held it next to my nose and sniffed. Daisies smelled like dirt.

"Save it until we get mayweed." She threw her arms around my legs and almost knocked me over. Nate was there that day and grabbed the flower and tossed it aside. Sparrow had cried until I picked a new flower from the bed and gave it to her.

I wished I'd kept the first flower.

Once back at The Nest, I cleaned up the tools I'd left lying around. Dad didn't like a mess. "This is my garage and my rules," He'd always said. "Tools get put away." *Not anymore.* These were my tools now. I tossed a wrench across the floor. Dad was gone. Mom was gone. Sparrow… I let a screwdriver fly, and it skittered across the cement floor, stopping in the exact place I'd failed her.

I gripped the edge of the top-heavy tool chest and turned it over with ease, sending sockets and wrenches in all directions before I slammed the door and ran upstairs.

I grabbed a beer from the refrigerator and plopped onto the couch. Nate was right. My life was shit. I could see it. He could see it. Even Mona the blind woman saw the truth.

I reached for my guitar. What would Sparrow look like today, had she survived? I strummed the chords without much thought. It was a song that played on a continuous loop inside in my head. Her laughter haunted my nights. The memory of her eyes haunted my thoughts. They were earth and sky no more. As a boy, I had pushed her away. As a man, I would never let her go. I loved her. I hated her. And twenty years later, I still mourned her.

Chapter 7

ANA

We sat in our favorite booth at Luigi's. Grace topped off her wine glass with a bottle that was already nearing empty and shook her head. "Fury is out in the middle of nowhere. What the hell are you going to do out there?"

"Stand on my own two feet, hopefully." I'd never been to Fury, so I had no idea, but I'd looked the town up on the Internet. There wasn't a Wayfair or a Coohills, but there was a diner, a mini-mart, and a liquor store. All I needed was ramen, wine, and a roof over my head. "I can't stay here. I'm being thrown out at the end of the month. It's a sign."

I was never one to put a lot of faith in signs, but an eviction notice followed by a house that now belonged to me seemed like a sign. A big sign. A neon blinking sign that shouted, "This way."

"It's a sign that says you're an idiot," Grace answered. "I told you that you could stay with me."

Staying at Grace's would be like staying at those hotels where they rented the rooms by the hour. She liked to "entertain" all the time. I'd spend my life on the couch with a pillow over my head.

"I've stayed at your house before, so I think I'll pass.

Remember Mark the moaner?" Lord, the man had sounded like a cat in heat with the way he'd screeched and howled. I'd sworn he would exit her room with his back torn to shreds, but the man had skipped his way to the door. His smile was like one of Grams' clowns. "Nope, I have to be an adult, Grace. I appreciate the offer, but I refuse to be a sadder version of Kramer from *Seinfeld*. At least he had a job."

"You're not tall enough, and better looking."

I twirled my spaghetti on my fork. "Thank God for that. If I were saddled with a face like him, I'd be in trouble." People could overlook my contacts, they could overlook my scar, but to have a face that looked like a terrier mated with a roach would be unbearable.

"Life comes in cycles. Yours is going to turn around. I promise."

"You forgot to take out your magic wand and sprinkle fairy dust over me." I cut the baseball-size meatball into pieces. "I need to move forward with my life. Stagnation leads to disaster. No job, no home, no man, no hope. Maybe this is how I work it all out."

"I could never move to a small town." Grace unbuttoned the top button of her shirt and looked around the room. "It would only take me a week to work my way through the single men."

I looked around the room, because I already knew Grace had scoped someone out. "Maybe you can give them an extra night or two, and it would take you twice as long to harvest the field of eligible bachelors." Her eyes kept drifting to a guy at the bar. Definitely her type. Blue suit. Blue shirt. Blue tie. The man was a human blue jay. "So, tell me who's on the menu this week, and don't say the guy at the bar. He's boring."

He glanced at her.

"You don't even know him." She licked her lips. The trap was set.

"He's wearing all blue. Lord, he probably has blue balls, too, which means he'll be a one-second man."

Her eyes tipped to the ceiling. "But he's wearing a Zegna suit."

I looked over to see that he'd turned toward us. "And a wedding ring."

"The good ones are always married." She poured the rest of the wine into her glass and caught the drop running down the bottle with her fingers. "Waste not—want not."

"Just don't fill up on the losers. There's a winner out there for you somewhere." I pulled the napkin to my mouth, then set it on the table. "I'll keep my eyes open in Fury."

FIVE DAYS LATER, I shoved my blowup mattress, TV tray, and lawn chair into the back of the Jeep. I packed up my clothes, along with the few belongings I kept of Grams', and headed toward Fury.

It was odd that Grams had never mentioned the property. Odder that we'd never driven to Eastern Colorado. Then again, she hadn't driven, period, but when Gramps was alive, we'd done some road trips to Pueblo and Taos. Never to Boulder or Vail or Breckenridge.

I took exit 134 and a sense of dread snaked out of my stomach. I would have closed my eyes like I did when I was afraid to see something, but I was driving, and my first encounter shouldn't be with the police.

When the road turned into Main Street, I slowed to a 35MPH crawl. I passed by a sign that read "Welcome to Fury." Whoever named this town must have had a chip on his shoulder. Who named a town Fury? It was like naming it "Rage" or "Anger" or "Wrath." With the colorful flowerpots hanging from the street's light posts, the place looked like something that should be called "Contentment" or "Cheer." In a way, I suppose Fury sounded cooler; it gave the town an edge of mystery.

To my surprise, the town looked cozy in a crazy off-kilter sort of way. It looked familiar, and yet it didn't.

My stomach growled, and I pulled into the angled parking space in front of the uniquely named The Diner. No confusing that for anything else, and with the sheriff's car in the parking lot, I knew it had to be good. If the locals ate there, then it was safe to say the food was okay. Then again, this was Fury, and The Diner was the only place to eat.

Inside the diner, a pretty blonde passed by and told me to sit anywhere I liked. I found my way to a side table that gave me a bird's-eye view of the place. To love a place was to know a place, and the only way to know a place was to pay attention, so I sat alone and watched life whirl around me.

"What can I get you to drink?" The blonde's nametag read, Hannah.

A picture of a thick chocolate malt decorated the space above my table, and I took it as another sign. "I'll have a chocolate malt."

Hannah rolled her eyes the way an irritated teen would. She took a side-glance at the booth up front. As soon as she saw the man sitting there, her look turned from resting bitch face to girl in love. "It'll take a while." She stared at me for a minute more, like she was waiting for me to change my mind.

I pulled my smile straight from my ass. "Extra malt, please."

"That costs more." At the back counter, she slammed an ice cream scoop on the counter.

Who cared if it was extra? I had several thousand dollars in my bank account thanks to Grams, and I was going to have a chocolate malt with extra malt if I wanted one. Off to the side, Hannah tossed the ingredients into the mixture like she was shoveling dirt into a pit. Then she finished it off with a disdainful splash of milk. The thought crossed my mind that she could poison me. She didn't have that girl-next-door demeanor. She was straight out of central casting for *Mean Girls*. Oh well, death by chocolate malt didn't sound all that bad.

I was in a new town with a new chance, and I even had a new home. Not to mention the man in the booth was cute, way cute, wipe the drool from your chin cute.

He turned my way as if he knew my eyes were on him, and my heart halted for a beat. He was more than handsome, he was familiar—and yet he couldn't be. Adrenaline raced through my veins until my heart rate rivaled a hummingbird's speed.

Hannah slammed my chocolate shake on the table in front of me. "The eyes are fine, sweetie, but keep your hands off, okay? Hawk is mine."

"Right," I said. "Not a problem." *Hawk?* Kill me now.

The burger and fries I ordered didn't please not-so-happy Hannah either. At least she didn't tell me the extra ketchup would cost more.

While I waited for my lunch, Hannah did her best to gain the attention of the man she called Hawk, but he didn't seem interested. Irritated was more like it.

The girl had excellent taste in men. I couldn't fault her for claiming him. He was tall, dark, and detrimental in one package. He screamed bad boy. That was apparent when the sheriff approached his table.

I heard something about a motorcycle, bits and pieces that sounded like threats. It was when the sheriff poked the man in the shoulder that Hawk let his hoodlum loose. It was like watching a dragon come to life. He stood from the booth and towered over the sheriff who, to his credit, didn't flinch but did rest his hand on his service weapon.

Hawk pulled money out of his pocket and threw it on the table.

"I'm watching you," the sheriff said in a deadly tone, one that could be heard clearly across the room. It was straight out of a horror flick. He sounded like the psychotic guy that calls the babysitter and says, "I know what you did last summer."

Hawk looked the sheriff in the eye. "Screw you." A man of few words, but clear and concise.

"I hate it when Junior is here." Hannah slid my meal on the table. "He's always on Hawk's ass." With a new attitude in place, she plopped into the seat across from me like we were friends. "You just passing through?"

"No, I inherited a house here on a street called Abundant." It was funny to look at my new address: 425 Abundant, Fury, Colorado. After seeing the sheriff and Hawk argue, I suspected that the address had painted an accurate picture. There seemed to be an abundance of agitation here in Fury.

"That neighborhood is a shithole."

Of course it would be a shithole. Nothing in my life came easy, so why not add in a place that was probably better off being condemned?

"It was mostly abandoned twenty years ago, but I heard they were auctioning off the property. Let's hope yours is livable." She smiled, but her sharp tongue lashed out. "If not, call me, and I'll put together a to-go meal for you to take with you on your way out of town."

"I guess I'll see in a few minutes whether I'm staying or going."

I used the last fry to mop up the pool of ketchup and then paid for my meal. I even tipped the blonde banty rooster well. I didn't need to make any enemies on my first day. That could wait until tomorrow.

Chapter 8

ANA

My Jeep squeaked to a stop in the driveway of the white house. Peeled paint and loose boards pulling away from the frame greeted me. The yard looked decent. At least it wasn't a suburban jungle like the house two doors down. That house was straight out of the movie *Jumanji* after the killer vines had taken over. My house looked deserted and unloved, but I could change that with a coat of paint and some flowers.

Would the interior have fared as well as the yard? My hope searching for a miracle, and the key gripped tight, I inched toward the door.

Bright sun, too long drive, a meal with an attitude from hell, I wasn't sure which caused the dizziness to hit. The house tilted on the flat ground. My stomach careened, and my heart picked up its pace. By the time I made it to the front porch, it was banging like a bass drum in my chest cavity. An overwhelming feeling of dread blanketed me. *What if it didn't work out here? What if I couldn't find work?*

I pressed the key into the lock, and it stopped at the first notch. I jiggled and pressed until it was fully seated into the tarnished brass knob. On the precipice of my future, I sucked in a lungful of air and courage. I had several thousands of dollars in the bank. I had a house. There were people with less who succeeded. I *could* do this. I *would* do this.

I turned the key in the rusty lock and pushed. Hinges creaked like they hadn't been oiled in years, and by the look of the place, that would be a generous timeline.

I stepped inside the almost vacant room. The same creak, reminiscent of a haunted house, sounded when the door slammed shut behind me. Light filtered through the tattered curtains. Cobwebs hung from the walls. If a voice echoed through the room that said, "Get out," my knees would buckle, and I'd die right there. But thank God, the house didn't have a voice—at least not an audible one. A silent voice spoke of abandonment and sorrow. Of a life cut short and dreams lost.

The living room floors were hardwood and covered by a layer of dust that billowed up with each step I took. Spiders scurried in several directions, leaving their tracks behind. Spiders, I could do. Rats, I couldn't.

I skimmed my fingertips along the walls. Dull paint that had once been yellow failed to brighten the space. The door molding was etched with faded lines. Crouching down, I traced the fading blue ink with my fingers. One year—eighteen months—two years—three years, and one line after that. Mr. Goodwin's words about the former owners dying hit me hard. Sadness squeezed the breath from my lungs. What happened?

A doorway opened into the kitchen, and I stopped. The place was a complete shithole, but it was my shithole. I flipped the light switch and waited. The old fixture remained lifeless, like the rest of the room. No buzz of a refrigerator compressor. No hum of a microwave. No whistle of a teapot. I didn't know what I expected. Abandoned homes didn't have utilities. Hell, some occupied homes didn't have gas, electric, or water if the tenant couldn't afford them.

When I blew the dust off the stovetop, I uncovered electric coils, and a song of thanks rang through me so deep, it vibrated in my heart. *Thank God.* That meant with the flip of a switch at the electric company, I'd be in business. Gas would be more difficult, since a house this old would probably need an inspection. My shoulders lifted. My heart rate slowed to a livable pace. Something was going my way.

Fury wasn't big, so my trip back was quick and double lucky, since everything was conveniently located. My first stop was the electric company. The woman was super nice and said she could put a rush on the order, which meant I was likely to have lights by nightfall. My second stop was the water department. After an older man named Harry finished flirting, he guaranteed I'd have water by the time I returned home. He also told me how to open the valves to start the flow and advised me to let the faucet run for several minutes to avoid getting sick. Stop three was the mini-mart. Nonperishable foods were a must in case the old refrigerator didn't function. Cleaning supplies and paper goods also hit the cart, along with a few treats like a candy bar and powdered donuts.

Nothing could motivate me like the smell of Pine Sol, and the promise of chocolate when I finished.

In the kitchen, I ran the water until it was clear like Harry suggested. The transformation started with a bucket of cold water and a sponge. I flicked the light switch on, but it was still dead, so I went straight to cleaning up twenty years of dust and dirt. I'd finished wiping off the flat surfaces in the kitchen when a knock on the front door echoed through the empty house.

Sweating and tired, I was in no condition to meet anyone. There was so much to accomplish before the sun went down. I brushed the sweat from my forehead and went to answer the door.

Standing on my porch facing the doorjamb was an old woman. She held a pitcher of lemonade and two plastic cups.

"Can I help you?"

She shuffled her feet to the left and faced me. Her white pin curls hugged her head tightly, and her near orange lipstick bled into the creases of her lips.

"Invite me in, dear. That's the neighborly thing to do because we are neighbors." She didn't wait for the invitation. She plopped her Clarks loafer on the threshold and heaved her body through the doorway.

When her shoulder hit my chest, I stepped back. "By all means, come in." It was a late invitation since she already stood in my living room.

"I brought lemonade. It's my special recipe. None of that powdered junk for me. This is made from lemons and simple syrup." She pressed the pitcher forward, but not toward me. Hastily, I grabbed the handle before she let go. She took off her dark glasses that nearly wrapped around her head and exposed eyes that were more silver than blue. "There you are." She turned to face me. "Damn eyes went to hell years ago."

"I'm sorry about that." I looked around the empty room. I had nothing to offer the old woman but a lawn chair.

Her squint became more pronounced, like she was looking through a pinhole, and I realized she probably was. Gramps had developed macular degeneration a few years before he passed. He, however, had never sported the dark glasses that were supposed to protect his remaining vision. He'd wanted to see what he could while he could.

"I have a chair for you here." I put my free hand on her arm and led her to the plastic seat. "It's not much, but it's all I have for now."

"Pour the lemonade. I want to hear your praises before I die." The old woman chuckled. "I'm Mona Charming. I live across the street."

Hopefully, that was her last name and not an attempt to sell me on her personal attributes. She needed to work on her social skills. Walking uninvited into someone's home wasn't exactly among Miss Manners' recommendations.

I offered her my hand, but of course, she didn't see the gesture, so I took the two red Solo cups she held. "I'm Ana Barrett, and I recently inherited this house." I filled a cup for Ms. Charming and one for me.

"I've been waiting for over a decade for this neighborhood to rejuvenate."

"Rejuvenate?" I sipped at the lemonade and puckered when the tartness hit my tongue. How good could lemonade made by a blind woman be? Turned out, pretty damn good. I drained the cup. "Delicious."

"I knew you'd like it. Everyone does." She looked around my house like she could see everything. As if reading my mind, she said, "I can still see what's important. For example, I can see this place is a total piece of shit."

Her bold demeanor was as refreshing as the lemonade. "You said something about rejuvenating the neighborhood. What happened here?"

"Nothing we want to dwell on." She waved her hand in a dismissive fashion. "Tell me about yourself." Elbows on her knees, she leaned forward and stared at me. "You're a pretty one." Her eyes focused on mine like they would tell her my story.

"Not much to tell." I slid to the ground in front of her and poured another cup of lemonade. "My name is Ana. I'm twenty-four. My Grams owned this house, but she recently passed, and I inherited the property."

"What was your grandma's name?" She pressed forward like she was going deaf, too.

"Agatha Barrett. She raised me after my parents died in a car accident."

Mona's shoulders sagged like she was weighed down with sand-bags. "Tragedy." She shook her head, and the little white curls bounced about. "Life has too much tragedy."

"I don't remember them, so it's not as big of a loss as everyone thinks. You can't miss what you can't remember. I suffered a brain injury, and maybe that was good. It would be hard to have a mangled heap of metal as my last memory of them."

"Enough of that. Let's talk men." She leaned back in the chair and braced her hands on her thighs. "It's been a long time for me, but I did like oral sex. Is that still a thing?"

Lemonade spurted out of my nose. "Umm …"

"Oh Lord, don't tell me you're one of those I'm-going-to-wait-until-I-get-married types." She snorted and moved her hands to my shoulders. "Take it from me. Try them all out. You don't want to open a bag of Skittles and only eat the green ones."

Laughter bubbled from deep inside me, but I swallowed the urge to set it free. "I don't like the green Skittles."

"Exactly, and if you hadn't tasted the green ones, you wouldn't know." She looked up to the cobweb-covered ceiling, but I was pretty sure she couldn't see anything. "You have to try them all until you find the one that tastes the best."

"Are we back to talking about oral sex, Mona?"

"Can we?" A glimmer of light sparkled from her silvery blue eyes.

"No," I said with more tenacity than tact.

"Fine." She let out a loud sigh. "Tell me more about you."

Grateful to be back on a topic that didn't include tongues and sex organs, I happily told her about myself. "I'm a graphic artist." I scooted back against the wall, creating a strip of dust-free hardwood flooring. "At least that's what I went to school to do. However, I haven't been able to get my business off the ground."

"We don't have one of those here, so I'm sure you'll be a hot commodity."

A loud chirping sound came from the fire alarm in the ceiling. "We have electricity." I hopped up and danced around the living room.

"Have we been sitting here in the dark?" She looked both ways, her brows nearly knitted together. She pulled a wristwatch the size of a wall clock to within an inch of her face. "Oh, thank the Lord, it's only three. Guide me to the bathroom, I drank too much lemonade."

I rushed to the grocery bag on the floor and pulled out the toilet paper. "Take this with you. The bathroom is the second door on the left." I pushed Mona in the right direction and stopped in my tracks. *How did I know that?*

I watched her shuffle down the hallway I hadn't explored yet. Mona walked into what I hoped was the bathroom and closed the door. If not, I'd be cleaning up after Mona when she left.

A few minutes later, she came out, wiping her hands on her pants. "You need a towel in there."

"I need a lot of things." The house was bare except for what I'd brought—and just bought—and that fit in the corner of my living room.

"I need to get home. *Judge Judy* has started." She headed toward the front door, and I got a feeling Mona saw a lot better than she let on.

"What about your lemonade?"

"You finish it up." She glanced around the room and shook her head. "What a mess."

Yep, Mona Charming saw a lot more than she wanted to admit to, but I liked her. She was at least entertaining, if not quite as charming as her name.

With its boxes of flowers in the window and pink yard flamingos, Mona's house straddled the line between cute and tasteless, but since I'd met her, my opinion leaned toward cute.

Chapter 9

RYKER

It wasn't the way I envisioned spending my morning, but it was time. Though it killed me spiritually to put a new throttle assembly on the bike, keeping the old one was guaranteed to kill me physically. I was adjusting the choke when the Skype tone on my laptop sounded.

Only one person ever Skyped me, so when I heard that sound, I rushed to answer the call.

"Dude, look at you." And every time I saw Silas, it reminded me of how much he had changed over the years. He was every bit the Army guy. His hair, once long, was now close-cropped and neat. His body, once lanky and lean, now rippled with the muscles of free weights and war. "You look good, man. How are things?" The screen shook, and his face came in and out of view. The connection was rarely great, but it was always good to see my brother.

"Hey there, Hawk." Silas leaned toward the screen so his face was dead center. He was only two years younger than me. There were days like today where he looked like a teenager. Other times, when life took a toll on him, he looked like an old man. Our early years had been tough, to say the least.

"What's up, Rooster?" Mom had given him that name because the minute the sun lifted, he was up and making noise.

"Oh, you know, different day, same shit. The normal early morning raids. The powdered eggs for breakfast. Showers that work on occasion. Toilet paper that feels like sandpaper on my ass. It's a damn paradise."

"Sounds like it." Silas' time was up soon. He'd been gone for nearly eight years, and I wanted him home. "You coming home this time?"

"Haven't decided yet." He pulled his hat lower on his head.

I could always read his eyes, so when he was warring with himself, he hid them from me. "The sex must be good in the field, or is that the goats I hear bleating in the background?"

"Screw you. I'd never nail a goat. Not saying it doesn't happen. Some of these guys here were raised on squirrels and possum. They would do and screw anything. What about you? Have you tapped that waitress yet?"

Dad's old office chair creaked when I leaned back and propped my feet on the desk. "You've been talking to Nate." Damn bastard was going to get my fist shoved down his throat. "I'm not doing Hannah. She's a forever girl. I know better than that. Forever is bullshit. All you got is now."

He yanked off his hat and stared straight into the camera. "All we got is now, and all you can promise anyone is the moment you're in. If you like her, go for it. Stop living in the past, man. It's eating up your future."

"Says the guy who lives on the edge so he can feel alive." I wished Silas hadn't joined the Army. He'd said it was because he had no options, and that was partly the truth. I had been rotting in prison when he turned eighteen. He didn't want to come back to Fury on his own. That might have been why he enlisted, but he stayed because it made him feel something. He thrived on the adrenaline. Making it through another day alive. That's what he took out of the massacre. He had an unquenchable thirst to live on the edge. "I want you to come home."

Silas shook his head. "Home? That hasn't been home for twenty years." Behind him, the Army green tent wall moved like a soft peaceful wave—flowing, traveling, in motion like my brother.

"It could be home. Mom and Dad built this place for us."

"Aren't you going to turn the shop into a bar?"

"Didn't qualify. No liquor license. No loan. Turns out, a gun isn't the only thing you can't have as an ex-con. What good's a bar without liquor?"

"Shit, that loan was supposed to help finance the private investigator."

I wrapped my hands around my head, feeling like my brain might explode. "I'm doing what I can." I'd promised myself I'd never let him down, but there I was, failing him. Again.

"It's not enough, Hawk. Our brother is out there somewhere. You talk about Mom and Dad leaving the place to us. Don't you think they wanted Decker to have a piece, too?"

"Yes, dammit, of course." Mom and Dad would have wanted us all together, but the system had other plans. Babies were easy to place, and Decker was adopted right away. I closed my eyes and saw his big blue ones. Mom called him Owl because his eyes were all you saw when you looked at him. "We'll find Owl, I promise."

Silas leaned back and propped his feet on the desk. The soles of his boots were caked with desert dust. "What do you hear from the private eye?"

I didn't hear from him at all. People don't work unless you have money, and money was something I didn't have much of these days. "I couldn't afford to keep him."

Silas picked up his cap and hurled it across the tent. "Then sell something. He's our brother. We've got to find him."

"Don't you think I know that?" I pounded my fist on the table, making the computer shake. "Don't you think if I could have kept him with us, I would have?" I raked my hand through my hair. "Aren't you glad we couldn't? Look at what happened to you."

"Don't you bring that up. I'm not going there ever again. Find something to sell. Do something." His voice cracked with emotion.

The day Mom had told me to watch my brothers and Sparrow, I had failed. I'd told Silas to watch Decker, and he believed he'd failed, too, but he hadn't. All of this lay on my shoulders. Every death, every life ruined was all on me,

"There's nothing left to sell. We might…we might have to give up the hunt for a bit."

"Bullshit. Do something." He flexed his fists, and I knew he'd be pounding a wall or something else to relieve the tension. "What about business? You're working, right?"

"I'm taking in any job I can. The problem is, the sheriff has chased out every biker within a twenty-mile radius."

"Screw the sheriff. From what you tell me, he's as bad as his dad was. What the hell are you doing with your time?"

"I've been fixing Dad's bike."

A glimmer of light reached his eyes. "You're going to sell it, right?"

My head reared back like I'd been slapped. "It's all we've got left of him."

"Stop making him look like some venerated saint. This is his fault. What parent brings their kids up in a biker gang, puts them at risk every day?"

I didn't have a valid answer. "When you're a kid, you don't know any different."

"You're not a kid anymore, and you know this was their fault. If Dad had been a normal father, we'd be living in suburbia while Mom made cookies and checked our homework after school. You blame yourself for what happened to them—what happened to us. It wasn't your fault."

"It was. You know what happened."

Silas growled into the screen. "I know you snuck in there, I know

Sparrow toppled a box. I know a bunch of trigger-happy assholes shot each other up. You didn't put the guns in their hands. You didn't pull the damn triggers. Sell that shit bike for what you can. I'll send you more money this payday. We have to find Decker."

I nodded. He was right. We had to find our little brother. "I'll do what I can."

"I love you, brother." Silas put his hand to the screen.

I pressed mine to his. "Love you, too. Come home." The screen turned black.

Back in the garage, dad's bike was in one piece. The throttle assembly in place. But Decker wasn't. Decker was gone. I hopped on the bike to give it a test run. It started on the first kick, and a throaty growl filled the air. At least something was working in my favor.

I turned out of the shop parking lot and accelerated down the straightaway. Seventy miles an hour felt amazing. The wind in my face, and the past at my back. I was free. Until I found myself back on Abundant Drive in front of *her* house.

I downshifted and came to a stop before the old, worn-out home. In the driveway sat a Jeep that had seen better days. There hadn't been a vehicle in that driveway since the murders, and this one didn't belong there.

A shadow passed in front of the bay window, and a feeling of ownership rushed through me. No one belonged here but *her*…and me. I closed my eyes and saw her twisted body as it bled out in front of my eyes. *This is her shrine.*

I vaulted off my bike and raced to the door. I pounded and pounded and pounded until a woman answered.

Her face was flushed with a smudge of dirt on her cheek. Long brown hair pulled into a ponytail hung over her shoulder. Her bangs stuck to the sweat on her forehead. She leaned on a broom and smiled like she knew me.

"Can I help you?"

"Who the hell are you, and what the hell are you doing in

there?" My words were harsh, and she was gorgeous, but I didn't care about either of those things. She was a trespasser. I wanted her gone, and I'd make sure she left immediately.

She stepped back from the door. "I own this place. It's my house."

"That's bullshit." I looked past her into the house that I hadn't entered in decades. "The people who lived here are dead."

She shook her head, making her ponytail swing over her shoulder to her back. "A lot of people who lived everywhere are dead."

"I want you to pack up your shit and leave."

Her mouth dropped open. "I'm not leaving. I legally own this piece-of-shit house, and I plan on staying." She gripped the broom handle and raised it like a weapon—a spear ready to stab me.

I smiled at her. Not a friendly smile, but the kind that says, *We'll see who wins this war.* She was crazy if she thought a broom handle would stop me from getting what I wanted.

"It is a piece of shit, so why stay?" I'd heard it was sold years ago, but to my relief, no one showed up. I figured it was an investor waiting for the right opportunity. This woman was no investor.

"Because it's my piece of shit, and it's all I've got. I'm not leaving, but you are."

She tried to close the door, but I shoved my boot into the opening. I knew I wasn't making as much sense as I'd like to. But what could I say? *I'm still sort of obsessed with the little girl who used to live here, the one I let die?* Instead, I told her, "You can't live here. Sorry, but that's the way it is." As if that made all the sense in the world. And then I fisted up and punched the door, leaving a dent and tearing up my knuckles.

The woman showed no fear; she stood her ground like a warrior. It was I who turned and walked away.

Chapter 10

ANA

I stared at the dent in my door. *Who the hell does this Hawk guy think he is?* It was bad enough the inside was a mess, and now the guy I recognized from the diner had to go and make the outside worse. With all my might, I slammed the door and hoped it wouldn't fall off the hinges. The entire wall shook, but the house remained standing. *Thank the Lord for small favors.*

And to think I found him attractive. I mean, he was easy on the eyes, but his personality was hard on the nerves. Hannah could keep him.

I stormed back to the bedroom to get the dustpan and stubbed my toe on a loose board. Super—another thing to go on my fix-it list. I hobbled back to the living room. If I wouldn't let a big bully stop me, I certainly wasn't going to let a sore toe slow me down.

I swept the last of the floor dust into the dustpan and tossed it into a nearby plastic bag.

This place was something of a lost cause, and it would take a lot of money to fix it up right, so for now, I'd fix it up livable. Thank God, the appliances worked. The old microwave hummed, and the lights dimmed when the refrigerator compressor kicked on, but they functioned. The appliances were nowhere near Energy Star rated, but they would see me through.

Hawk's voice replayed in my head, telling me I didn't belong here, and he was probably right. This town had nothing to offer me except shelter. Half of me wanted to call Grace and tell her to get her couch ready. The other half of me wanted to make it work.

Obviously, Grams had kept this house for a reason. Somehow, she'd known I'd need it, and I wasn't turning my back on her gift. Grams had never had much money, so buying this place had been a big deal, and I wouldn't toss the gesture away simply because a brute of a man said I didn't belong. I'd prove him wrong.

Determined not to let that asshole ruin my day, I grabbed my purse and hopped in my car. Nothing made me happier than paint, so I headed to the hardware store to pick up a can or two. A coat of happiness could wash the sorrow from these walls.

Grace always said that a house had energy, and that was something this house lacked. It had died with its owners. Wasn't it time to breathe some life back into it?

Ten minutes later, I drove down Main Street again. There was Fury Liquor, Fury Laundromat, Fury Dry Cleaners, Fury Grocer, and The Diner. I walked into Fury Hardware. It would be hard to get a design job here when everything was the same; then again, they could use some good branding. I had a feeling Fury would be feast or famine. I'd keep my mind focused on abundance.

"How can I help you?" A guy leaned against the register with his hands tucked into the front pockets of his jeans. He was handsome in a frat boy kind of way. He looked preppy, but there was something underneath that said he could pull off the bad boy, too. There was a hint of mischievousness in his eyes.

"I'm looking for paint."

He pushed off the counter and walked toward me. "You came to the right place. Are you new in town?"

"Yes, I just moved in." I looked around for the paint. "Do you do custom color?"

"Finally," he said. "We got the machine a year ago, and no one's asked me for anything but white paint. I'm Nate, by the way." He walked in front of me, signaling me with a crooked finger to follow. "I'll make any color you want except white."

On the back wall was an entire display of color samples. It didn't take me but a minute to decide on a butter yellow. It was darker and richer than the color on the faded walls, and it was sure to lift the spirit of the house. When I woke up to the color of sunshine surrounding me, I'd certainly feel happy.

"I'll take three gallons of this, and I need a gallon of white trim paint."

He gave me a dirty look. "I'll give you white only because it's for trim. What else do you need?"

A million dollars. A job. A real bed. Those were things I wanted, but they weren't necessarily what I needed. "Do you know someone I can hire to help do some minor fix-ups to my house?" Obviously, any handyman in town would get his supplies from Fury Hardware.

"I've got a buddy who has some time and could probably lend a hand." Nate shoved the three cans into the mixing machine and pressed start. In less than five minutes, the paint was finished. It was going to be a great upgrade. I needed cheap fixes, and paint was the easiest and least expensive way to transform a space.

I rushed around the store, grabbing other things I needed, like a tarp and brushes and a roller and tape. I spent a few more minutes looking at things I could only dream about. New light fixtures. New faucets. Hinges to replace the rusted ones in the kitchen. I brushed across a cloth shower curtain decorated with pretty sunflowers but chose the clear plastic curtain because it was only two dollars. I picked up several bottles of acrylic craft paint and a few decent brushes. I couldn't afford art, but I could make art.

Nate rang up my purchases, which came out to be over a hundred bucks. I wrote down my phone number and address so he could put his friend in touch with me.

We lugged the buckets to my car. As I was about to put the last one in the back seat, I heard the rumble of a motorcycle and looked up to see Mr. Not So Congenial pull into the hardware store parking lot.

My feathers were still ruffled from our earlier encounter. Seeing him again so soon made me burn beneath my skin. There was no way I could leave things the way they were. That man had vandalized my home.

Dropping the bucket none too gently, I stomped toward him, leaving Nate at my Jeep.

Chapter 11

RYKER

I felt her before I saw her. The hair lifted on the back of my neck like it did before a storm.

I'd pulled into the hardware store parking lot to see whether Nate wanted to grab a quick lunch when she came rushing toward me like a rabid pit bull with her teeth bared.

"You owe me, asshole." She had her finger pointed at me like she was identifying me in a lineup. "You damaged my door with your stupid meaty fists." She came closer, and now that pointy finger poked me in the chest. I had to give her credit. She was bold. Not many people had the courage to do that to me.

I grasped her hand, and she gasped. I didn't squeeze her hand, but I held it against my chest to stop her jabbing. "Calm down."

Her mouth dropped open, giving me a glance at her slick pink tongue. A tongue I was sure to get a lashing from any minute, and not the kind of lashing I preferred.

She ripped her palm from my grip. "Calm down? You're telling me to calm down? That's rich coming from a guy who punched my door. *My* door, asshole. The door on *my* house. I should call the police. There has to be some law against vandalism, even in a podunk town like Fury." She stomped her feet and fisted her hands against her jean-clad legs. "God, I feel sorry for your girlfriend."

I shook my head because I had no idea what in the hell that meant. *What girlfriend?*

She turned and strutted back to her car. The engine revved and kicked up gravel as she tore out of the parking lot.

Nate walked up to me, laughing. "Making new friends, I see."

"Shut the hell up, Nate," I grumbled. I didn't need his shit. "You coming to lunch or not?"

"Yeah, I'm coming. Just let me tell my dad." Nate turned to leave.

"Bring your wallet. You're buying because you pissed me off." I climbed back on the bike and waited.

He turned around to face me and walked backwards. "She pissed you off. Maybe she should buy."

"Hurry up, I'm hungry."

Nate took off on a run and returned a minute later. He climbed into his truck, and I followed him to the diner.

Good ole Hannah was all smiles when we arrived.

"Two days in a row. How did I get so lucky?"

I pushed past her, but I heard Nate say, "Since when do you consider bad luck to be lucky? Bring him an iced tea. He needs it to cool down."

I slid into the corner booth and hunkered down. It had been a shitty day. I should have gone right home, but after my talk with Silas, I needed to clear my head. Next time, I'd know to go straight back to bed rather than heading out to create a clusterfuck.

"What did you do to that girl?"

Before I could answer, Hannah plopped two iced teas on the table and her ass on the bench next to me.

She leaned over and put her head on my shoulder. "You want some sugar?"

She wasn't asking about the kind that came in packets. The girl had been openly offering me her sweets all year.

I pressed my finger against her shoulder until I made her sit up straight. "What I want is a burger and fries."

She let out an exaggerated sigh. "And you?" She looked at Nate.

"I'll take some sugar if you're offering. I get off at five."

She reached across and palmed his cheek. "Sorry, Nate, you're sweet enough on your own." She turned to look at me. "This one, though, he needs all the help he can get, and I'm pretty sure my sugar can make him sweeter."

"I watch my sugar intake, sweetheart. Don't want to risk the chance of diabetes."

She pushed on my shoulder. "You're an asshole, Hawk."

I grabbed her arm before she could get up. "To you, I'm Ryker. You haven't earned the right to call me Hawk."

She pulled her arm from my hand. "Who pissed on your Wheaties this morning, Ryker?" She said my name with exaggerated flair.

Nate laughed. "Some new chick that moved here is twisting his nuts."

Hannah moved to Nate's side of the booth. "She was in here yesterday. Plain and mousy looking, right?"

"Wrong girl." There was nothing plain and mousy about the girl I'd met. She was a freaking goddess covered in dust.

"In all fairness, it's a matter of opinion. When I looked at her, I thought she was cute in that kind of lost puppy way. She was definitely a six or seven, but when she ordered colored paint, she moved up on the beauty scale to a high eight." Nate held up ten fingers, then dropped two.

Hannah grumbled. "I'd give her a five at best."

"Don't you have a job to do?" I said and stared in her direction.

Hannah lifted from the booth and walked without urgency to the kitchen.

Nate leaned in toward the center of the table. "What happened with you and Sunshine?"

"Who the hell is Sunshine?"

"The chick from the hardware store. She bought yellow paint. It reminded me of the color of sunshine."

"Storm is more like it. She's like a damn hurricane." I pulled four packets of sugar and dumped them into my glass. I stared out the window for a minute. "She moved into Sparrow's house."

Nate almost dumped his tea over. "No way. It's about time, man. That neighborhood has been a graveyard too long, don't you think?"

"I can't let it go, Nate. I can't let *her* go."

Hannah came by and literally tossed our burgers in front of us. When she turned around, she flipped up her skirt, giving me a view of her barely covered ass. It was a nice ass, but it wasn't for me. Asses like that came with commitments and expectations. I had enough shit on my plate; I didn't need to add more.

My phone rang. It was the private eye that I'd called before my fateful motorcycle ride. "Hey, Henry, thanks for calling." He asked if we could meet at the garage. "Give me twenty-five minutes."

"News on Decker?" Nate shoved a handful of fries into his mouth.

"I don't know, I called the guy and told him to start again. He said he might have found a break in the case. We'll see. The problem is, each time he goes in search of a break, it costs money, and I'm out of money."

Nate dropped his burger and leaned in. "I almost forgot. Little Ms. Sunshine needs cheap labor to help fix up her house."

"Are you crazy?" I bit off a chunk of burger and dumped a blob of ketchup onto my plate. "The woman hates me."

"Get over it. It's easy money, and you need money. She needs cheap labor, so I'm pretty sure she can overlook your faults."

I took a few more bites of my burger before wrapping it in a napkin. "Not happening. I don't want her in the house in the first place. I'm not going to make it easier for her to live there."

"If she has a deed to the property, there's nothing you can do about it. Isn't it time to let it go?"

He was probably right, but I wasn't in the mood to listen. "I've got to run. Thanks for lunch." I pulled a few more fries into my mouth and headed for the door.

My bad luck to have Sheriff Stuart pulling up as I was leaving. The asshole never left me alone.

"Savage," he said as he exited his cruiser. He always used my last name like they did in prison.

I nodded and kept walking toward the bike. The fries stuck like dried toast in my throat.

"That thing registered?"

I swallowed hard. "Yep, all legal and everything. You'll have to try harder, Sheriff. I've been a law-abiding citizen for years." I had no real choice. The man was like an enema.

I shoved the napkin-wrapped burger into my pocket and started the bike. A minute later, Sheriff Stuart was in my rearview mirror, and the woman in Sparrow's house was on my mind.

I pulled into the garage parking lot in time to see Henry arrive. The scarecrow of a man climbed out of his car. He always smelled like cigarettes and bad coffee. I supposed it was a hazard of the job.

"Hey, Henry." I killed the engine on the bike and hopped off.

"Don't you wear a helmet?"

I ran my fingers through my windblown hair. "Not always. Sometimes it's nice to have the wind dry my hair. Besides it's not required in Colorado."

Henry took a last puff on his cigarette and tossed it to the ground. He ground the ember to death under the rubber sole of his tennis shoe. "You know they sell hairdryers everywhere."

"That shit's for girls." I walked past him and into the garage. "What do you have for me?" We stepped over the tools and made our way to the office. I pointed to the old foldout chair in front of the metal desk. It was the chair I used to bend over to receive the lash of Dad's belt when I misbehaved.

Henry pulled out an invoice. "I need a retainer to continue." He slapped the page in front of me. "I know you're tight on money, so I made half due now and half due in thirty days." He pointed to the line that read one thousand dollars.

"I've paid you thousands of dollars already, and I have nothing to show for it." I wanted to boot kick the man straight out of my office or bend him over the chair and give him the end of my belt, but I kept hearing Rooster's plea. We had to find Decker. He was the only family we had, and finding him was a priority. "Okay, so as soon as I give you five hundred dollars, you'll dig in?"

"I've got a lead. I found a person who worked at the Department of Social Services when your brother would have been placed. I want to talk to him to see if he can put us in the right direction."

"All right." I looked past the man's balding head through the window of my office to my dad's old Harley. "I've got to sell a few things, and then I'll get you the money. Give me a few days." Months ago I would have been able to write him a check, but since Stuart had been harassing the bikers that came through town, they didn't tend to stop here anymore. I'd taken to fixing anything with a small engine. My life had gone from fixing Harley Davidson bikes to lawn mowers and vacuum cleaners.

I stood up and showed Henry to the door. As soon as he cleared the property, I went to my computer to email my brother.

Rooster,

I talked to the private eye. We've got a plan. I'll let you know when he starts up again.

Hawk

There was eleven and a half hours' difference between Colorado and Afghanistan. I wasn't sure whether he'd be up this late, but soon enough, the ding of an incoming message sounded.

Hawk,

I know how hard that will be for you, but you know our parents would want us together. It's too bad you can't pick up some side work.

Rooster

His mention of side work made me think of the house on Abundant. Maybe it was time I started acting neighborly. Maybe it was time I offered my services to the new owner. Maybe it was time to let it all go.

Chapter 12

ANA

I sat on my lawn chair and scrolled through the classified ads. After waking up on the floor for the second time in a row, I needed to do something about my sleeping situation. Surely, someone had a gently used mattress for sale.

Looking at the house was almost too much to handle, but I remembered Grams always telling me there was only one way to eat an elephant, and that was one bite at a time. This house was the equivalent of an elephant, or maybe a herd of them.

I followed my index finger down the ads with no luck and then turned to the jobs section. Although I wanted to pursue At Flight Graphics, I'd take any job at this point. Sadly, there wasn't much open in Fury. The sheriff's department was interviewing for new officer candidates, but I was pretty certain I didn't want to enter law. I fell into a fit of giggles imagining myself toting a gun when my phone rang.

Grace's ringtone was *Man Eater* by Hall & Oates. It had seemed fitting at the time I got the phone. Hell, it seemed fitting now.

"Barrett Residence," I said with a deep English tone. "This is her butler speaking."

Grace laughed, which was my intent. "How's life on the other side?"

"Still living the dream. I've managed to fit all of my furniture in the house. There was a problem with the bed, though."

"Too big for the space?" She knew I was sleeping on a twin blow up air mattress.

I rolled my eyes, even though she couldn't see. Somehow, it made talking to her feel like she was right next to me.

"No, it was perfect, but it appears that inflatable beds and nails sticking out of the floor aren't a compatible mix. How are you?"

"I feel like shit. I've been home in bed for the last few days." I could hear the ice machine plunking chunks into a glass in the background. I had an ice machine, too. It was my hands rotating the plastic trays so they would release the big fat cubes.

"Say it isn't so. No happy hour at Wayfair Lounge?"

"There's nothing funny about being sick. I've been puking up my guts for three days. I wanted to lose ten pounds, but not by eating saltines and drinking mint tea. You're lucky you got out when you did. The plague is upon us."

"I told you to get your flu shot. With the number of men you swap germs with, you're like a walking host." I padded barefoot to my window and looked across the street. Mona was sitting on her porch, drinking what looked like coffee. I'd have to pop over and say hi later.

"I don't think it's the flu, I think it's something I ate."

"You mean someone you ate." I laughed so hard, I hit my head on the window.

"You're awful to me. I don't even know why I'm friends with you."

"Because you love me. Besides, I think you're allergic to not having me around."

"I think that's truer than you think it is. I miss you. Tell me the truth. Is it awful there?" I could hear the concern in her voice, and there was no way I was going to make her worry more on top of being sick.

"Actually, I like it here. It's different."

"Any hotties?" Of course, that's what Grace would focus on.

I thought back to the men I'd met so far, and one came to my mind. Dark hair. Blue eyes. A giant of a man. "No, not really. There's a guy named Nate that works at the hardware store. He's nice enough, but not my type." I pulled my cup to my mouth and took a sip of cold coffee.

"Still holding out for a hawk?"

I choked, and the coffee squirted out my nose. "I met one. Not particularly a nice guy, but his name was Hawk."

"No freaking way. Oh my God, Ana, it's providence."

"All right, Jane Austen. I told you this guy wasn't particularly pleasant."

"Neither was Mr. Darcy when he met Elizabeth Bennet, and do I have to point out that your name starts with *A* and hers started with an *E*, both vowels? Her last name was Bennet, and yours is Barrett, which is almost the same. This is total kismet."

"Oh yes," I said with as much sarcasm as I could fit into two words. "Seriously, it's all good here. I'm going to start painting today. I'm scouring the want ads for a bed and—"

"Gross, you can't buy a used bed."

"Why not?" I left the window and walked into the kitchen to make myself another cup of instant coffee.

"Because other people have slept and done other *things* on it." She sounded mortified, her voice lowering to a whisper as if she were in a crowded room and talking about a venereal disease.

I filled my cup with water and stuck it in the ancient microwave that shuddered to life when I pressed start.

"You've stayed in a hotel. People have slept on those mattresses and have most definitely done other *things*. What's the difference?"

There was a moment of silence on her end. I'd made her think.

Knowing Grace, she'd be black lighting the mattresses of the hotels she stayed at from this point forward.

"It's perception. I expect that when I pay two hundred dollars a night to stay at a higher-end hotel, they take the necessary precautions."

I placed a heaping spoonful of coffee into my cup and stirred.

"Yep, they change the sheets." I pulled the creamer out of the refrigerator and splashed a dash into my cup.

"That makes me feel sick to my stomach."

As I was about to respond with something witty, my doorbell rang. Who knew I had a working doorbell? "I've got to go. Someone is at the door. It's probably my blind neighbor."

"Wait, you have a blind neighbor?"

"I'll call you soon and explain. Feel better. Love you." I hung up the phone and raced to the door. It would be nice to chat with Mona. At least she was entertaining.

I swung open the door with a big smile on my face, only to find the man called Hawk standing there.

I tried to shut the door, but he leaned in so I couldn't. The man was built like a brick wall.

"What are you doing here?" I stood in front of him dressed in nothing but flannel shorts and a tank top. His eyes skirted my body, and my nipples pebbled under his gaze. In my rush to cross my arms, I forgot that I carried a cup of hot coffee, and it splashed across my chest. The burn of the liquid was nothing compared to the burn of embarrassment that washed over me when I looked down to see I'd unknowingly entered a wet T-shirt contest. "Wait here," I snapped, then turned and ran toward the room where my clothes still sat in a box in the corner.

The door closed, and I prayed that he had the decency to leave, but his heavy footsteps crossed the living room floor. Today wasn't my lucky day.

Once I was dressed in jeans and a sweatshirt, I faced my unwelcome visitor. He stood in front of the window. Slivers of light broke through the branches of the tree out front and caused prisms of colored light to dance on the walls. One prism created a halo around the man's head, but I knew better. This man was no angel.

"Now that you've damaged the outside of my house, are you back to do a job on the inside?"

He swung around to face me. God, he was beautiful. Dressed in dark jeans and a cotton shirt that strained across his chest, he reminded me of a biker minus his leather cut. I'd always had a thing for the bad boys. Grams had called it a phase. Grace called it bad taste. I called it attraction. "Why are you here, Hawk?"

His eyes narrowed at the use of his name. "My name is Ryker. Ryker Savage. Only those who have intimate ties call me Hawk." He looked around my house like he was seeing it for the first time. "What's your name?"

"I'm Ana. Ana Barrett." I should have offered him my hand to shake, but this man set my nerves on edge. He didn't scare me as much as intrigue me. And he infuriated me more than that.

"Nice to meet you, Ana." He walked past me into the kitchen. "Nate tells me you need a handyman."

I rushed after him. "Yes, but not you." The man must have had an aneurysm while he was yelling at me yesterday. He'd been all about throwing me out then, and now he was ready to fix up my place so I could stay.

He stopped in front of the sink and tightened the faucet to stop the drip. "I'll work cheap. I'm good with my hands, and I know this house better than anyone." I didn't miss the flash of pain that crossed his face when he mentioned the house. He obviously had ties to the people who used to live here, but that didn't make him qualified to work for me.

He brushed past me and down the hallway. "Where's your furniture?" He stepped into my bedroom and looked at the puddle of blue plastic on the floor. "That's your bed?"

I rushed over and picked it up. Once rolled into a ball, I shoved it into the closet. "It was. It experienced a death by nailing."

Was that a smile that broke his stern expression? His eyes lit up when he smiled. It was like a light behind his irises went on and the blue glowed brighter. "I can probably help with that, too."

I bet he could. After the way he looked at me, I didn't want to get anywhere near a bed with him. "I appreciate the offer, but I'm not equipped to deal with the whole multiple-personality-disorder thing."

He looked at me with confusion, and then I saw it dawn on him. "I'll fix the door. No charge."

"I'll take you up on that, but I don't think we're a good fit for the rest. I'll find someone else."

He turned and walked down the hallway toward the door. When he passed the doorjamb that was marked with ink lines, he stopped, lowered onto his haunches, and skimmed the marred wood with his fingertips.

"Did you know her?"

He bit his lip and nodded his head. "Yes. I killed her." He sprang up and rushed out.

I stood there, stunned. Surely, he didn't mean he murdered her.

Chapter 13

ANA

I woke up on a pile of my clothes to the persistent sound of banging. I would have sworn it was coming from somewhere else until I heard it directly outside the wall of my bedroom. I flew up from the floor and stomped outside.

On a ladder, pounding in loose nails on the siding was Ryker.

"What the hell are you doing?"

He climbed down the ladder and stood in front of me. The man towered over me by at least a foot, but I'd never been one to back down. Grams always said I was three parts angel and one part demon. Today I was in touch with my darker self.

"I'm working on your house."

"I didn't ask you to work on my house." I put my hands on my hips and realized I was standing in my yard dressed in nothing but a T-shirt and Hello Kitty underwear. I looked up. Ryker hadn't missed my lack of clothes. "Stop looking at me."

He laughed. "It's hard not to look at you. You're nearly naked."

"I'm not naked." From across the street, I heard Mona laugh.

"Even she can see you're nearly naked, and she's almost blind." He pulled off his flannel shirt and wrapped it around my shoulders, covering the parts that were facing the street but leaving my front exposed to his eyes.

"You need to leave. You're trespassing." I pulled his shirt closed in the center. It smelled like dryer sheets and spice and him. "I can call the police."

"You could, or you could let me work for you. I could use the work, and you could use the help."

"Yesterday, you told me you killed a girl." I shivered thinking about it. Ryker didn't seem like a murderer, but Jeffrey Dahmer probably seemed pleasant before he killed and ate his victims.

"I didn't murder her, but I feel responsible. It's not something I want to talk about. But in full disclosure, I spent six years in prison for murdering the asshole that abused my brother, and I'd do it again." He stepped away from the ladder. "You either want my help or you don't. I'm not going to beg you for the job."

There was something different in the way he reacted this time: desperation paired with resignation, which I understood completely. It was the same way I'd felt when I had to come here. I wasn't entirely comfortable with the idea of him working on my house, but he was right; I needed something he was offering.

"You can stay, but I'm paying you half of what I was going to pay the guy at the Handyman Connection. That's twenty dollars an hour, and you better work fast because I have more work than I have money."

His firm jaw twitched as he gave me a thin line of a smile. Not the type of smile that said he was happy, but the type that said he would take whatever he could get. "Deal. I'll finish up out here, and you can tell me where to start inside the house." I turned around to walk away, but his next words halted my progress. "Nice pussy…cats."

I pulled his shirt down as far as I could and took off toward the door.

I didn't dare shower with a strange man around the house—especially one with a temperament that blew in different directions. One minute he was a gentle breeze, the next he was a tempest.

Instead, I pulled a pair of jeans from my makeshift bed and grabbed a T-shirt. I lifted his flannel shirt to my nose one more time and inhaled his scent before I let it slip to the floor. There was something unsettling but oddly comforting about the way he smelled. A chill skirted through my body—a cross between fear and arousal. He was definitely my type physically, even if he was something of a douchebag.

While he fixed the loose nails on the siding, I started painting the living room. By lunchtime, I was done with two walls and starting on the third when my stomach grumbled in complaint.

I pulled out the bread and made two sandwiches. I tried to convince myself that it was only polite to offer him lunch, since I was paying him less than what his labor was worth.

I found him around the back of the house. Not a place I'd investigated yet, but it was in as bad of shape as everything else. Decades of neglect had killed off the grass, and only weeds remained, but at least the yard wasn't overgrown. Someone had obviously done some yard work in the past.

I stood at a distance and admired him. Every swing of the hammer caused his muscles to bunch and ripple. His broad back tapered to a slim waist, and his jeans hugged his thighs like a hungry lover.

As if feeling my stare, he turned and looked over his shoulder. I stepped forward, hoping I looked like I was in forward motion instead of at a standstill, caught gawking at the hot bad boy on the ladder. "Hey." I held up a paper plate filled with a bologna sandwich and chips. "I thought you might be hungry." He shifted his body and looked at me like I was offering him a petri dish filled with Ebola. "It's a bologna sandwich."

He backed down the ladder with speed and efficiency. In seconds, he was facing me with a smile. Not a smile that said, *cool, a bologna sandwich*, but a smile that said I was giving him much more than a free lunch. Too bad everyone didn't light up like that over two slices of bread and a piece of mystery meat.

I turned to walk away.

"You're not going to make me eat alone, are you?" he asked.

What the hell was he about? He was like a teeter-totter at the playground—up and down constantly. He confused me. He intrigued me. He caught my attention.

"It's not like I have a chair to offer you. I've only got one. If you want to eat together, we need to sit on the porch." I made my way to the front porch and took a seat on the top step. Ryker followed and sat on the step below me. Even at that position, he towered over me.

"Tell me why you're here." His voice wasn't angry like it had been yesterday, but confused. And why wouldn't he be baffled? I'd showed up out of nowhere with nothing.

"My grams died and left me this house. I was struggling to make ends meet in Denver, and my options were limited. It was come here or sleep on my friend's couch." I shrugged and looked down at my meager lunch offering. It wasn't much, but it was all I had. It was sad that the sum of my worth was limited to the contents of my refrigerator and the clothes that lay scattered in the bedroom of my run-down house.

"At least at your friend's, you had something to sleep on."

He popped a chip into his mouth, and I watched his lips move as he chewed. Red ruby lips that looked soft and kissable. *What the hell am I doing? The man has a girlfriend. And he's a psycho.* Those were passing thoughts, though; I gripped onto the fact that he was so yummy to look at. This girl needed to glom onto any positive moment, and having Mr. Dark and Dangerous sitting on my porch was about the nicest thing to happen to me in a long time. *How sad is that?*

"One thing at a time. First is making sure the house isn't going to come down around me. I'll worry about comfort later." I took a bite of my sandwich and enjoyed the silent companionship for a moment.

We both sat looking across the street toward Mona's empty porch.

"Have you met Mona?" He set his empty paper plate on the step above him and wiped his mouth with the bottom of his T-shirt. When he pulled it up, I caught a glimpse of his stomach. Ropes of well-defined muscles bulged and rippled with the movement. When he dropped his shirt, he gave me an I-caught-you-looking smile.

Heat rushed to my face. I looked away and toward Mona's bungalow. "Yes, she's a hoot. I'm not sure what to make of her yet. Yesterday, she wanted to talk about lemonade and oral sex." I slapped my hand over my mouth the minute the last two words were out. "Shit."

Ryker lifted his eyes with interest. "That sounds like Mona. Did you?"

"Did I what?" I crumpled my empty plate and set it on top of his.

"Talk about oral sex?"

I leaned away from him, as if being close to him was like taking a lie detector test. I didn't know why I'd told him that, or why I wanted to tell him anything he wanted to know. Was it because I was lonely, or was it because for some strange reason he seemed familiar?

"No, I didn't talk to Mona about oral sex." He watched my mouth as I said the words, and I swear there was heat in his eyes. "We talked about the shitty condition of my home, and how it had been abandoned for twenty years."

Ryker's expression hardened. Gone was the warmth, and in its place was a thick dark heaviness. It cloaked him anytime the house was mentioned. He had gone from approachable to shut down.

It probably wasn't smart, but I needed to know more about him. If he was going to be working for me, I needed to feel safe, and Ryker didn't make me feel safe. It wasn't that I was afraid of what he could do to me. He was a fortress of a man, but it was his silence and anger that sliced at the raw edges of my nerves.

"Hey, can you handle coming here every day? It clearly made you insane the other day."

His eyes were large, glittering ovals of sadness. His shoulders rounded enough to cast a gloomy shadow on the sidewalk. "I knew the people who used to live in this house, and things didn't end well for them." He scrubbed his hands over his face, as if the action would erase the memory. "Sorry about my behavior."

I could tell by his tone that he didn't want to continue, so I backed off and replaced the thousands of questions racing through my head with a declaration.

"Let's turn this place around. Help me take it from a place of despair to a place of delight. Deal?" I seemed to be making a lot of deals with Ryker lately.

He didn't say a word, only nodded his head and left me sitting alone on the porch while he returned to work.

Ryker left shortly after lunch and returned with Nate and a bed.

"Where did you get this?" I stood against the wall while they put the frame together.

"I had an extra at my house." They lifted the box spring and mattress into place, and I almost cried. I had a bed. A real bed. I hadn't had one since I left Grams' house. "I brought sheets, too." He tossed the flowered fabric onto the bed and walked out of my room.

Nate stared at me for a moment. "Thanks for hiring him. He needed the job."

"What's his story?"

Nate shook his head and walked toward the door. "It's not mine to tell."

I heard the door close behind them, and the engine of Nate's truck rumbled to life. I stood and stared at the bed. I'd won the damn lottery.

Once the sheets were on it, I fell back onto the soft mattress and thought about Grace. She'd be appalled that I'd accepted a used mattress from a stranger. I curled on my side and thought about the quiet, stoic man who gave me this wonderful gift. Did his body ever lie on these sheets? Did the frame ever squeak under his weight? I buried my nose into the linen and inhaled. It smelled like fabric softener and him.

Chapter 14

RYKER

I'd been working on Ana's house for a week. The outside was all nailed back together, and the inside was coming along well. It pained me each time I walked inside the place, but every day the pain lessened as I saw her put every ounce of energy she had into redeeming the place. In some way, fixing the house was helping me, too.

By the fifth day, her house was almost furnished. I emptied my home and filled hers, but the stuff I brought took on new life the moment it entered her home. The drab brown sofa looked like warm milk chocolate in her place. The leather chair my dad would sit in at the end of the day made a perfect place for her to sit back and read.

Each layer I peeled from my existence and brought into hers was like a weight lifted from my chest. The things that reminded me of my family pressed down on me in my home but buoyed my existence when placed in hers.

She breathed new life into everything. I even brought her the old metal desk from the garage, and she painted it to look like a masterpiece. It was where she set up her computer and stacked the books she found at the thrift store. Little by little, the abandoned building had become a home.

The Skype ring had me racing toward the empty office. I hit the answer button and watched my brother's face filter through the choppy screen. I slid to the floor and pulled the computer onto my lap.

"Hey," I said. Happiness pulsed through me.

"Where are you at?" Rooster moved his head like he was trying to look behind me.

"I'm in the office." I lifted the computer and gave him a panoramic view.

"It looks different." A question lingered in his eyes. "You remodeling?"

"Yeah, asshole. I'm adding a Jacuzzi and a sauna for when you return." I wanted him to return. I missed him more than was manly to admit.

"No, really, what's going on?" He shifted and put his arms behind his neck. He was always in motion. Silas was a live wire that needed a constant supply of energy to keep him going.

"I gave the desk away."

"Dude, you could have sold it and used the money for the investigator." He lunged forward and brought his face close to the screen. "We need to move forward. We're running out of time."

"I'm working on it, but I keep thinking, what if he's got a good life? What if finding him messes him up somehow? What if he's better off without us?"

Silas pushed off the table and rocked his seat forward so he was inches from the screen. Close enough for me to see the shadow of his unshaven face. "The fact that you're asking that question means he wouldn't be better off not knowing us. We're family, and family sticks together. Now tell me why you gave Dad's desk away."

How did I explain my insanity? "I've been working for the woman who's living in Sparrow's house. She had nothing, so I shared what I had with her. No use having things collect cobwebs here when they could be useful someplace else." I leaned back and rested my body against the wall. "The shit in this house isn't worth the time it would take to place an ad, but she appreciates it, and I like feeling appreciated. Besides, she paid me for the first week, and it was enough to put Henry back to work."

When my brother smiled, I followed with a grin that hurt my jaw.

"What's she like?"

I tried to act nonchalant about her, even though the mention of her made my pulse quicken. She'd worked herself inside me somehow. She started out as an annoying splinter under my skin, and now she was the force that held me up most days. She gave me purpose.

"She's a woman who needs help. There's nothing special about her." Could my brother see the lie in my eyes? Everything about Ana was special. Not special in the way Sparrow was, because Sparrow was bigger than life. Death had a way of making people remember things differently from the way they actually were. I'd turned Sparrow into a saint of a child, when in truth she was a precocious brat, but I loved her spirit, and in some weird way, Ana reminded me of her with the way she didn't back down, and the way she fisted her hands on her hips and stomped her feet when she got frustrated.

"I'm calling bullshit. She's done something to you. Have you nailed her yet?"

I sat up tall and nearly knocked the computer off my lap. "No, it's not like that." Not that I hadn't thought about what it would feel like to sink myself into her body. I'd spent all week thinking about it, but I couldn't. She was exactly like Hannah in a totally different way. She would expect more than I could give. She would want something I didn't have to offer—my heart.

"You sure light up when you talk about her. Remember when Stacy Hammond showed you her boobs in junior high? You had a smile a mile wide for a week. I'm seeing something different in you. Like maybe a hint of happiness."

"Shut up, loser." I tried to look serious, but I couldn't. A broad smile took over my face.

"Screw you, and please screw her. I think it would be good for you." Silas tilted his head like he'd thought of something. "She's not like an old lady, is she?"

"No, she's young. Like in her twenties."

"Ugly?"

"No, she's hot."

"Fat?"

"God, you're an asshole. She's got all the right stuff in all the right places." I licked my lips, thinking about her in that kitty cat underwear and the look on her face when I'd told her she had a nice pussy...cat.

"Yep, I'm definitely calling bullshit. You need to tap that, and quick, before someone else in town does."

The thought of anyone else with Ana stirred something unpleasant inside me. My fists ached to connect with the face of whomever that someone could be.

There was a ruckus in the background, and Rooster said he had to go. The feed cut off before I could say goodbye. It weighed heavy on me to let him go. He lived in a war zone, and every call could be the last. Thankfully, this one ended on a good note. *When was the last time Silas and I laughed and joked?* It had been too long.

THE NEXT DAY, Ana put me to work in the kitchen. She wanted to take the hinges off the cabinets and spray paint them to remove the rust. Thinking that things would go faster if we moved on it together, we worked side by side. I used good old-fashioned brawn and a screwdriver to remove the hinges. Ana tried using the drill in reverse.

I stood back and watched her line up the screwdriver head to the hinge and then press the button. The thing took off like shrapnel from an explosion. She ducked, and the hinge crashed against the wall behind her, leaving a dent in the drywall.

I laughed my ass off as she looked at the screwdriver, the hinge, and the ding in the wall. "Great, another thing I have to fix."

My belly hurt from laughing. With my arms wrapped around her, I positioned my body behind her and held her hand. "You need to torque it down so it spins slower." I turned the knob on the drill and showed her how to click it down into what I'd describe as a lower gear. I leaned into her so we touched everywhere we could, and it was so damn good. "Some things are better done with slow precision."

My mouth was close to her ear, and her body shuddered when I spoke. I'd seen her look at me. It wasn't the look of a woman without interest. She ate me up with those big brown eyes of hers. "You can make it come…out better if you take your time." I was playing with fire here. I knew it, but I'd be damned if I could help myself. Ana was the first woman I'd felt anything for that wasn't simply a twitch in my pants. I liked her. I liked the way she challenged me. It was like she had an internal bullshit meter, and she wasn't putting up with any of mine.

She turned and looked over at me. We stared at each other for a beat too long, and I leaned in to touch my lips to hers. As the heat of her lips brushed mine, a knock came on the door, dragging us out of our moment.

Ana broke away from me, but not before looking at my lips. Was that regret I saw on her face? Regret that we almost kissed, or regret that we didn't get to?

She rushed from the kitchen to the living room to answer the door.

Chapter 15

ANA

My fingers went straight to my lips as I walked to the door. The heat burned deeper than the surface he touched. He twisted and fired up my insides, but I wasn't that girl. I mean, I was. I wanted him with every cell of my body. He was a bad boy, dark and brooding. He was exactly my type, but he wasn't mine. He had a girlfriend, and I refused to be anyone's deep, dark secret.

I threw open the door, expecting to see Mona or Nate, but it was Grace in tears on my front porch.

"We need to talk." I stepped back and let her into my home. She looked around the place and smiled through her tears. "You're such a big, fat liar." Her words weren't said with any hint of seriousness, but her tears continued to fall. "You said you lived in a hovel." She spun around and looked at my mostly furnished house.

"I've been lucky to have some help." I ushered her to the sofa where she fell into the cushions like she was worn through and through. "What's going on?"

The sound of the drill echoed from the kitchen, and Grace lifted herself from the couch. "Who's here?" She swiped at her tears and pinched her cheeks. Leave it to Grace to find energy when it came to meeting new faces. Male faces, that was.

"It's the handyman."

She straightened her clothes and headed in the direction of the sound. She made a dead stop in the doorway.

I had to admit, he was a sight to see and had stopped me dead in my tracks a few times as well. I could stand around and stare at him all day, but then I'd never get anything done.

"That's a tall piece of man candy, isn't it?" she asked, looking over at Ryker.

"He's taken," I said. Ryker balked, but before he could answer, I pulled Grace into my bedroom and shut the door. "I can get you a glass of wine." It was one of my guilty pleasures. I rewarded myself for a day's work well done with a glass of wine and sometimes a few ropes of red licorice. Most people liked to pair wine with a meal, but I treated it more like a dessert event.

Grace shook her head no, which was odd because I'd never known Grace to turn down wine of any kind.

"I'm pregnant." She flopped onto the bed and cried. In-between her tears, she got out the rest of the story. "He's married." She wiped her runny nose with her sleeve. I came to sit beside her, and she buried her face in my lap. "He's the only one I broke my no condom rule with. And that only happened once."

"It only takes once, Grace. What were you thinking?" I ran my fingers through her hair.

"I wasn't thinking. I was feeling, and my hormones overrode my brain."

"What does he have to say about the situation?"

She rolled over and looked at me with her bloodshot green eyes. "He told me to get rid of it."

"Who the hell is this asshole?"

Grace covered her face with her hands. "My boss," she said in a muffled tone.

"Shit, Grace, what are you going to do?"

"I don't know. That's why I came here."

I folded my arms around her and hugged her tight. "You can stay here while you figure it all out."

THE NEXT MORNING, Grace and I drove into the booming metropolis of Fury. Traffic was backed up by one car at the only stoplight in town.

"Don't tell me this is it." She twisted in her seat to look behind her.

"No, there's the diner up ahead, and Ryker owns a motorcycle repair shop on the opposite end of town." I made a left at the light and pulled into the parking lot of the diner.

"I can't believe anyone can live out here. There are no bars, no men."

I looked down at her flat belly and shook my head. "Men are what got you in the situation you're in now."

She lowered her head. "I know, but not all men are bad, just the ones who sleep with you on their lunch hour and go home to the wife at the end of the day." She twisted her lips into a frown. "I thought he was different."

"He was—he was married." I turned off the engine and twisted in my seat to look at her. She looked better today. After a night of crying, she had it all out of her system, and she could plan her next move with a clear head.

"He didn't wear a ring. He never talked about a wife. I had no idea."

"Would it have mattered?" Grace worked hard and played hard; when she wanted something, she'd pursue it with single-minded focus until she claimed it.

"Yes, it would have. I've never knowingly slept with a married man." She opened the door and stepped out.

Grace's words were always picked with care. She said she wouldn't knowingly sleep with a married man, but then again, I wondered whether she ever asked.

We walked into the diner and found Hannah glaring at us. Mostly at me, because she'd never met Grace. "Sit where you want," she said with a sigh. She was a pretty girl, and I could see why Ryker was with her, although they never looked together. Ryker didn't seem like a warm-and-fuzzy kind of guy unless he was whispering in my ear. The thought of that sent shivers all the way to my sex.

When I thought of Ryker, which was always, I imagined he was more of a get-in-and-get-out kind of person. I didn't see him being all lovey and romantic. I saw him as the kind of guy who didn't mince words. He and Hannah probably had an agreement. He gave what he wanted, and by the look on her face anytime he was around, it wasn't enough.

We ordered breakfast, and I drank coffee while Grace drank juice. She was a woman with child now, and her choices were important. I wondered whether my mother had been extra careful with her diet while pregnant with me. I had so many questions that would forever remain unanswered.

Grams had told me how pretty my mother was, but she didn't have many pictures. In fact, she didn't have any of my father. They hadn't been married, and I got the impression that Grams didn't like him much. She blamed him for my mother's death. He was driving, so according to Grams, it was all his fault. I closed my eyes and focused on pulling a picture of them into my memory like I'd done a million times before, but nothing came. Nothing ever came.

"Is there anything to do out here in the boonies?" Grace asked as Hannah brought our food.

"There's a carnival in the next town over. It's happening tomorrow night. You should go."

"Are you going with Ryker?"

"Right." Hannah turned and left without offering any more.

"Is that what hicks do for fun?" Grace asked once Hannah left.

"Hicks and pregnant women," I laughed. "We're going."

Chapter 16

RYKER

"I don't know why you brought me here," I said, shaking my head.

"Because you need a change of pace."

Nate and I walked from the parking lot toward the Ferris wheel. "My pace is fine."

Nate stepped in front of me. "Yeah, if you're a sloth. Seriously, man, you need to get out more often. I'll give you credit for working at Ana's house. I didn't think you had it in you."

"I have a lot in me you don't know about." I'd known Nate for the first eight years of my life. Then everything changed. Hospital. Foster care. Prison. It was all a damn disaster.

"I'd love to listen to you if you ever want to talk about it. What happened when you left Fury?" He stuck his hands in his pockets and walked beside me.

I was a human time capsule, and I wasn't sure I was ready to be opened, but I knew that bottling up the rage and anger and guilt wasn't helping me either.

I turned right and walked into the beer tent. I slapped a twenty on the counter and bought my friend a beer. Working at Ana's had put me in a better financial situation, and I owed Nate a drink or two. He was the reason I hadn't starved the past few months.

We took our red cups to an open picnic table and took a seat.

"There's too much to tell, but I'll give you the shortened version." I sipped at the suds that floated on top. They were hollow bubbles that reminded me of my life. I hadn't really lived since I was eight. I'd been on some kind of survival mode. One that got me through a day at a time but never allowed me to experience anything besides sorrow, regret, and rage.

"I'll take any version. You're my best friend, and I want to know what happened to you."

I set the beer on the splintered wooden table. A lump formed in my throat, and I swallowed it down. I was familiar with that lump. It threatened to choke me every time I thought about the early days after my parents died.

"After the hospital, I went to a temporary family. Olga and Cecil Gates cared for us until the system placed us. Once we were taken from them, we were transported to Denver." I closed my eyes and remembered the ride. Silas, Decker, and I were in the back seat, together for the last time. Decker was in the car seat, and I watched him gurgle and coo contentedly. He was still a happy baby, having no idea how much his life had changed. He was an orphan, but he didn't know it because someone was still feeding him and changing his diapers. "We went into a group home. Silas and I did, but Decker was put with a separate family. Turns out our group home didn't take children under the age of five. That's the last day I saw him."

"Shit, man, I had no idea. I thought you were all together at first. I mean...I know he was taken away, because you've been searching for him forever."

I nodded, reliving the pain of finding out that Decker had been adopted. "We didn't have any relatives willing to take us on. Mom was an only child, and Dad was the black sheep of his family. In their eyes, we were tainted by him."

"Assholes." Nate sipped his beer and looked over the edge. I knew he wasn't satisfied with the little I'd told him, but it was more than I'd ever divulged. Living with the memories was like tearing out stitches with my fingers. It was bloody and painful. "How many places did you and Silas end up?"

I mentally counted the families in my head. "Five. I had an anger problem that most couldn't deal with. I took my frustration out on drywall and doors and windows." I thought about Ana's front door and shook my head. Obviously, I hadn't changed my mode of expressing anger.

"At least they kept the two of you together." He pushed my beer toward me, and I took a long gulp. The bubbles burned as they traveled down to my stomach.

"They tried to split us up at first, but Silas ran away from two homes trying to find me. The social worker gave up, because chasing my brother took too much time and she was lazy." I drew circles in the condensation on the cup. "The day he walked into the Mitchells' house was the best and worst day of my life. We'd been in the system for years by then, and Troy Mitchell was a mean bastard. He never touched me because I was meaner than he was, but when Silas showed up, he knew he'd be my weak spot."

Nate looked sideways. This was where it all got uncomfortable, because this was where my life took a straight dive into misery. Troy Mitchell's house made hell look like heaven, and he made Satan look like a saint.

"You'd think they wouldn't allow someone so mean to foster kids."

I rolled my eyes. Sure, there were some great foster families out there—people who thought more about the kids than the money they got for housing and feeding them—but the Mitchells weren't that family. In the system's eyes, they were great. They housed the maximum number of kids and received the maximum compensation. It afforded them a big house and fancy cars. The money never went to the kids. They marked off the criteria of housing, clothing, and feeding us, but they didn't care for us. They only cared about that next check.

"To the unsuspecting social worker, they were the poster children for being the perfect foster parents. None of their kids got into trouble. No one ran away. When interviews were done with the kids, they all bubbled about how great Troy and Amy were. They were afraid to tell the truth."

"What about you?"

I considered his question for a moment. "I didn't say anything after the first time." I pulled up the sleeve of my shirt and showed him the burn marks on the underside of my arm where the sensitive skin was puckered in red circles. A perfect row of five. Troy liked the number five. Five burns. Five punches. Five kicks. Five days without food. Five hours in the snow without a coat. *Asshole.*

"I thought those came from prison or maybe injuries from the garage after the…" His head fell forward. This was hard for him to hear and harder for me to say, but something had happened over the past few weeks. I'd opened up. I'd shared my things and my life with others, and I felt better somehow—lighter and less stressed. Stronger. I hoped by the end of this, I'd feel empty in a good way. Empty of the pain I held inside. Empty of my self-loathing. Empty of guilt.

"Nope, it was all him." We sat in silence for a minute. People walked around us, laughing and goofing around. I couldn't remember a time when I felt free enough to be like that. I wanted to have fun. It was time to finish the story and move forward. "We'd been with the Mitchells for years, and Silas took a lot of punishment for being my brother. The Mitchells explained his black eyes and bruises by saying he was an active child."

I shook my head, remembering that last day. "I'd come home with a less-than-straight-A report card. Troy was pissed because somehow my B in algebra reflected on him. He sent me to my room, which was fine, but he locked me in and I heard my brother screaming." I shuddered at the memory. "I got out of there by breaking through the door. It's amazing what a chair can do when mixed with rage."

I took a big gulp of my beer and crushed the empty cup under my palm. "I raced toward the screaming and found Troy in his room with my brother. He was beaten and bloody. Silas's eyes were vacant, and I knew he'd been abused in the worst way. Everything went black for me. I know I beat Troy. I know he fought back, and the last thing I remember was pushing him out of the second-story window and watching him fall to his death." In the end, Troy had won that fight because I'd gone to prison for six years for second-degree murder.

"You got a shit deal."

"Actually, I got off pretty good with six years. After he was dead, the rest of the kids came forward with the truth. They told tales of beatings and abuse that would make most adults shudder. The home was shut down, and the kids farmed out to other places. Silas was sent to a family who was good to him. They were military, which is why he joined the Army. He still stays in touch with them."

I rose from the table and looked down at Nate, whose face was almost white. We'd never talked about the details of anything. Not the garage, not my life after, and not prison, but somehow it was right to let it out tonight. Empty the emotional coffers to allow room for fun. "Enough shit for one night. I'm ready to have a good time. Now tell me again why we're here."

"We're here to get laid. Carnivals are the best place to find chicks, dude. It's the bumper cars. It shakes them up just right. Leaves them dying for a touch."

"You're an idiot," I told him. "I can't believe I listen to you."

But he wasn't listening to me anymore. "Oh, cheese fries!" Nate practically ran to the vendor. I rolled my eyes at how easily he was distracted—or was he looking for a quick exit from the darkness?—but I liked cheese fries, too, so I followed him.

From there, we moved to the booth where a person was supposed to throw a ring around a bottle to win a stuffed animal. I'd never tried to do it, but I was sure the bottlenecks were too big for the rings. How else would they make money? I watched person after person put their money on the counter and fail.

"You call this fun?"

"At least we've got cheese fries." Nate held up a plate full.

"Give me that." I pulled them away from Nate, and they went flying through the air and right onto the blouse of a woman passing by…a woman who happened to be Ana.

Chapter 17

ANA

Grace and I had almost reached the midway when a plate of cheese fries flew through the air like an errant missile and crashed into my chest. Warm, gooey cheese ran down the neckline and settled between my breasts. Grace stood back and laughed, then she did the unthinkable. She pulled a fry from my shoulder and dipped it into the cheese on my neck.

"Manna from heaven," she said.

I gave her a dirty look.

"What? I'm eating for two, and I'm hungry." She reached to grab another fry, but I swatted her hand away. *Who in the hell throws food at unsuspecting people?* I scoured the area around us, and my eyes landed on Ryker and Nate, who stood wide-eyed and silent next to the ring toss booth.

Dust kicked up around me as I stomped toward them. Nate took the coward's path and hid behind Ryker.

"Did you do this?" I pointed down to my chest, which was a big mistake because it only focused his attention on my nipples, which puckered and pebbled underneath the thin cotton.

Ryker smiled as he locked his eyes on the pert nubs pushing into the fabric. "I hope so," he said in a cocky way that sent shivers down my spine.

"You're impossible." I turned around and marched toward the food tent, where they were bound to have napkins. I wiped at my chest until most of the cheese was gone, but it was useless. My pale pink shirt was now stiff with coagulated cheese and orange oil stains.

When I looked up, Ryker stood in front of me wearing nothing but an open leather jacket. A large tattoo I couldn't distinguish crossed his upper chest. He held his plaid flannel shirt out as a peace offering. Behind him were Grace and Nate, who were talking animatedly as if I hadn't received a cheese shower.

"I think you owe me some cheese fries," Ryker said.

My jaw almost hit my chest. "You're kidding, right?"

He pushed his shirt into my hands and wrapped his arm around my shoulder. "Yes, I'm kidding. Now let's get you changed before the rodents take notice and begin to swarm around you en masse."

At the mention of rodents, I happily followed him.

He walked me toward the outhouse while Nate and Grace walked behind us, still deep in conversation.

Once inside, I removed my shirt. It was a total loss, so I tossed it into the trash bin.

I brought Ryker's flannel shirt up to my face and inhaled his scent. Clean. Fresh. Manly. I slipped my arms inside and rolled the sleeves up a few times, but they still hung below my hands, and the length dropped down to my knees. There was no doubt that I looked ridiculous. Maybe like that kid in the movie *Big* when he returned home in the suit made for a man.

My hands ran softly through my hair, and I pinched my cheeks to rosy them up. I didn't know why, but I wanted to look presentable for Ryker. Despite our rocky start, we'd developed a friendship over the past few weeks. Once I'd gotten past his disagreeable behavior, he'd turned out to be a decent man.

He waited for me outside the restroom and laughed at the way his shirt swallowed me up. How could it not? He was built like a Mack truck, and I was built like a Mini Cooper.

"Let me help you." He walked forward, and I noticed how he'd zipped his jacket halfway up, leaving a peek of tattoo showing on his chest. It was a shame, because I could have looked at his abs all night long. They were their own kind of entertainment. In fact, I'd bet women would pay to sit and watch his abs. They could line hunky men up and call it something like "The Ripples and Ridges Revue." I'd certainly pay for that show.

"Haven't you helped enough?" I said without a hint of agitation. I was happy Ryker was here, and judging by the look on Grace's face, she was getting on well with Nate. It wasn't the I'm-going-to-eat-you-alive look that Grace normally gave men. This was different, and I was glad. Maybe she'd learned something from her less-than-desirable situation.

"Let me fix this," he said. He reached for the hem of the shirt, and when he got both ends in his hands, he tied it at my waist, then went to work on the sleeves. Somehow, he cuffed the fabric and then buttoned the wristband over the mass so that the sleeves fit me, in a way.

"How did you know how to do that?"

He shrugged and said, "We got a lot of hand-me-downs as kids. I got good at making things work."

"I'd love to hear about that sometime."

He weaved his hand under my arm and led me toward the rides. "Someday I'll tell you."

We waited in line at the Ferris wheel, because that was the only thing Grace could safely ride. When it came time to get on, she jumped ahead of me and climbed into the car with Nate, leaving me alone with Ryker.

"You can thank me later," she yelled as her car moved up, and the next car became available for Ryker and me.

"After you," he said with a flourish of his hand. I entered first, and he followed.

As each car filled with passengers, we lifted higher into the air. It was late May, and the air was crisp and cool. I wrapped my arms around my body, feeling the chill run through my bones. Before I knew it, I was leaning into Ryker, trying to steal some of his heat.

"You cold?"

My teeth chattered. "Freezing."

"I'd give you my shirt, but I already gave it to this cute thing who spilled cheese all over herself."

With indignation, I sat up straight. "Is that how you're playing this? You're going to pretend you didn't lob a plate of cheese fries in my direction?"

He laughed, and it was good to hear him laugh. It wasn't something that happened often, and I liked the sound of him happy. In fact, I liked it so much that I decided to make it my mission to keep him laughing.

"It was an accident."

"The least you could have done was offer me a wiener." The words were out before I processed them.

His eyes glittered with humor. "I'm still happy to offer you a wiener, if that's what you want." He lifted his arm around my shoulder and pulled me to his side. "How about we start with getting you warm?"

Little did Ryker know, but I was already sizzling hot for him. My insides burned while the frigid night air cooled me from the outside. Hannah was a lucky girl. Or was she? She wasn't here with Ryker tonight, I was. It wasn't a date—he had come with Nate—but why had he left her at home? I wasn't going to ruin the moment by asking. Maybe they weren't exclusive. I shook that thought straight out of my head once I replayed Hannah's words: "The eyes are fine, sweetie, but keep your hands off, okay? Hawk is mine." Those were exclusive words.

The Ferris wheel went round and round until it finally slowed to a stop, letting Nate and Grace off. She looked up at us and saw Ryker's arm around me, and she smiled. I shook my head, trying to tell her she had the wrong idea, even though deep inside I wished it were different. Fury, Colorado, would be a different experience if I was sharing it with someone, but I wasn't.

Grace cupped her mouth and yelled up at me, "Nate is taking me to the diner. I'm hungry for real food. I'll see you at home." She gave me a wink that I'm sure no one missed and pulled Nate in the direction of the parking lot. That poor man didn't know what hit him.

"Looks like we're on our own," Ryker whispered in my ear. "What's next?"

I had lots of nexts that I'd rather do with him, but I pointed to the Scrambler, and that's where we went once we got off the Ferris wheel.

What was I thinking? The Scrambler was a brain-bruising ride that threw me in several directions at once. When we got off the ride, I was happy that I hadn't eaten anything prior. I looked up at Ryker to see whether he was rethinking his cheese fries, but he didn't show anything beyond pure exhilaration on his face. It was like this was his first carnival.

Like a kid, he raced me from ride to ride, trying to get it all in before it shut down for the night. A light mist started to fall, causing my skin to chill.

"One more thing, and then we'll go." He sounded so excited that I didn't have the heart to say no, even though my feet ached and my body was numb. "Let's go in here."

We stood in front of the mirror maze. The roadie took our tickets, and we entered alone. Most people sought the adrenaline of the rides, so the mirror maze, in my experience, was often overlooked.

We walked around, trying to find our way out, but the maze was unforgiving. We found ourselves walking in circles until Ryker got the crazy idea to split up.

He headed to the right and pointed me to the left. "Last one out is a rotten egg." It was such a childish thing to come out of this big man's mouth, but I was never a quitter, and I loved a challenge.

"You're on. Loser buys our next meal."

He yelled over his shoulder, "I already got you cheese fries." Then he disappeared.

There were a million mirrors around me. All reflections of me. I saw myself from every angle. It was when I didn't see myself that I knew I was going in the right direction. Up ahead, I saw the reflection of a man, but it wasn't Ryker. To my right, I saw a woman that I didn't recognize. Behind me, faces flashed in the mirrors, but no one was there. My heart pumped at a pace that left me dizzy. My mind played games with me. I saw Grams and Gramps. I saw my mother and a man with blond hair who looked familiar, but I didn't know who he was. I saw a baby and a row of motorcycles. I heard screaming, but there were no voices. My blood pounded out a rhythm that was almost deafening. I grabbed my head and slid to the ground. I'd never experienced such terror in a place that was supposed to be fun.

I called out his name. There was no answer, so I yelled louder. Still nothing. I closed my eyes. Blood. Shattering glass. It all played like a movie behind my eyelids, and I knew I'd remembered my past. Not the good memories like baking cookies and finger-painting, but the crash that took my parents away, and all I could do was cry.

Curled in a ball against a mirror, I waited to be saved. I kept my eyes closed, afraid of what I'd see in the reflection of the mirrors.

"Ana, are you okay?" Concern filled Ryker's voice. On his knees in front of me, he wiped the tears that fell from my cheeks. "What happened?"

I took in a choppy breath. "I don't know. I couldn't find my way out, and then the mirrors …"

"What about them?" He pulled me into his arms and lifted me to my feet.

"They showed me things I couldn't remember. I saw the car crash that killed my parents. Glass and blood were everywhere." I covered my face and sobbed.

Ryker pulled me close and held me until I stopped blubbering. "It's going to be okay. Memories are like that. They attack you when you're not expecting them. Let's get you home." I nodded into his leather jacket, then looked up into his face. What I saw there melted me. He cared. He knew what I'd experienced. The pain of his own torment was written all over his expression. He stared at me, and his eyes softened. When his lips came down to claim mine, I didn't hesitate to kiss him back. I needed his comfort. I needed his strength. Something told me he needed the same.

His tongue stroked mine in a delicious way that sent the fear away and replaced it with desire. He explored my mouth like he was searching for something more, and I wanted him to find it there, but then I thought of Hannah, and I was mortified. I wasn't *that* girl. Realizing what I'd done, I pushed him back and turned to walk away, but I twisted my ankle and fell to the ground.

"Shit, shit, shit!" I yelled and grabbed my right ankle.

Ryker was back on his haunches in front of me.

"What's wrong? Why did you turn and run?" He looked like I'd slapped him in the face. "Was it the kiss?" There was a silent hurt that faded his blue eyes.

"I shouldn't have kissed you. You have a girlfriend. I'd never make a move on someone else's boyfriend."

Ryker's expression was priceless. It was like I'd told him the sky was green and the grass was blue.

"What the hell are you talking about?" he asked. "I'm not with anyone, and don't you dare apologize. I liked the damn kiss." He picked me up and carried me through the maze. When we got outside, he set me down and asked for my keys. "I'm driving."

I handed them to him without argument. My right ankle ached when I put too much pressure on it, and pressing on the gas pedal for the next thirty minutes didn't sound appealing.

He offered me a piggyback ride, but I declined. The kiss was tempting enough that I didn't need to wrap my legs around his waist and have my girly bits pressed tight against him. I limped all the way to my Jeep while he scowled at me.

Ryker looked like a badass, but he acted like a gentleman. He opened the door and lifted me inside, even though my ankle was feeling much better. Once I was buckled and safe in my seat, he made his way around the car. I stared at him every second, wondering what was happening between us. He was a man of sharp contrasts. One moment he was sunshine, and the next a thundering storm. He was sweet and savage. Saint and sinner. Sexy and sinful. And he was single. That bit of information made me smile.

He climbed in and adjusted the seat to fit his long legs. The engine choked and sputtered, then finally growled to life. "When was the last time this thing had a tune-up?"

I gave him a confused look. "Huh?"

He shook his head. "You've got a lot to learn. Let's start with some facts. I'm not anyone's boyfriend. Where in the hell did you get that idea?"

I shifted in the seat to face him. His profile showed a nose that had been broken more than once. His jaw was strong and covered in a shadow of facial hair that gave him a rugged look. He was the hawk I'd been looking for, and now that he was single, maybe he could be mine.

"Hannah told me that you were hers."

Ryker's hands gripped the steering wheel. He shoved the car into reverse a little too roughly and backed us out of the parking space. "She's a handful, that girl."

It wasn't my business, but I wanted to know. "Have you ever been with her?"

He gave me a quick sidelong glance. We were moving forward, driving down the highway toward Fury. Big raindrops hit the windshield. He flicked on the wipers, and they screeched with every swipe. "You need new wipers, too."

It didn't escape me that he hadn't answered the question. I turned and looked out the window. We sat in silence for seemingly a lifetime until he finally answered my question. "I've never been with her. Not one kiss, one feel, or even a quick lay."

I snapped my head in his direction. "Then why would she say that to me?"

"Because she wants it to be different." He turned toward me. "You're the first girl I've kissed in months, and I plan to do it again the minute I get you home."

Not wanting him to see the desire in my expression, I turned around in time to see a cow in the center of the road.

Chapter 18

RYKER

Ana's scream was the only thing that saved us from hitting that damn cow. As soon as she turned, her hands came up to protect her face, and I knew we were on a collision course with something. Thankfully, quick reflexes made me swing right, just in time to clear the beast. If anything, we gave it a close shave with the bumper, but by the way it was sauntering down the wet pavement, I guessed we'd missed it completely. It walked away. The same couldn't be said for us. We barreled at fifty-five miles an hour into a wet field.

"Are you okay?" I unbuckled my seatbelt and leaned over to check her out. My hands skimmed her body, making sure she was in one piece. She felt good under my palms.

I couldn't believe I'd crashed her Jeep. Having just relived her parents' death in the maze of mirrors, I was certain she'd be a wreck, but she wasn't. Maybe she was in shock.

"Oh my God, we almost hit a cow. Do you know how long we could have eaten on that roadkill?" She wiped her forehead with a shaking hand.

"I'm trying to make sure you're okay, and you're talking about a side of beef?"

She unbuckled her seatbelt and turned toward me. "Two sides of beef. I swear that was a whole cow in the middle of the road, but I haven't been seeing things clearly tonight, so maybe it was a half a cow. And…if that's true, then we have bigger problems than running off the road."

"You're crazy, but you make me smile." I reached over and cupped her cheek like it was a natural thing to do, and she leaned into my touch.

"What now?" She wrapped the flannel shirt around her fisted hand and wiped the fog from the inside of the window.

I could tell by the sucking sound around us that we were stuck in the mud. Even in four-wheel drive, the wheels kept spinning. I dropped my hand and reached into my coat pocket for my phone.

"I don't have a signal. Do you?"

Ana reached inside her purse for her phone. She pressed in her security code, and the screen lit up. "No bars here either." We were almost to Fury, alone on a stretch of mountain road that sat between two mountain peaks and was deserted except for a few ranch homes that dotted the flats in between. Of course we didn't have a signal. I shouldn't have been surprised. Life was anything but easy. At least that was my experience.

The engine had died the minute we came to a stop. I turned the key over and over, but it barely gave me a sound. "Looks like we're stuck until someone finds us." She wrapped her arms around her body and shivered. Without the engine running, there wasn't a heater. I leaned over the center console and tried to wrap my arm around her, but it was awkward and ineffective. There was too much space in-between us. That's when I got the great idea to climb into the back seat.

"You're joking, right?"

"No, if we sit close together, we share body heat. Someone is sure to find us soon." I wasn't sure whether that last part was true, but I didn't want her to be frightened or cold. I climbed into the back seat first and patted the space beside me. "Until then, let's stay warm."

She gave me a wavering glance before she relented and climbed in back beside me. "Grace will come looking for me if I don't show up at home."

"Super." Though now that she was next to me, I wasn't sure how super that sounded. Being alone with Ana in the back seat had a certain appeal. I wasn't so sure I wanted to be found right away. I lifted up and leaned forward to turn off the headlights shining across the field.

"Shouldn't we leave those on?" She curled into my side and laid her head against my chest. This was heaven. I knew I had nothing to offer this girl but misery, but I didn't care. For once, I was taking something for me. Life could piss off.

"They're at the diner. It will be at least an hour before they start looking for us. We'll turn them back on later. I'd hate for the battery to die before then." It was a good lie. Sounded believable to me, and it must have to her as well, because she nodded and scooted in closer. The windows fogged around us, and I moved in for the kiss I had originally planned to take once I got her home.

Within seconds, she was on my lap with her hands tucked under my leather jacket. My hands were in her hair. Our lips pressed together, and my tongue explored her mouth. She was sweet, warm, and inviting.

My erection pressed against her bottom, and each time she moved, I swore under my breath.

She pulled her lips from mine. "Am I hurting you?"

"You're freaking killing me, but I'll die happy." I lowered my hands to grip her ass and pulled her into my rock-hard rise.

"Oh..." She lifted her hips, but I pulled her back down onto my hardness. I loved the friction her body created. It turned out the back seat was a brilliant idea. My skin burned, and by the rocking of her hips against me, I was certain she wasn't focused on how cold it was.

She didn't put up a fight when my hands slipped under the shirt and seared a path up her bare back. In fact, her moan told me she liked the way my calloused fingers touched her skin. It had been a long time since I'd had my hands on any woman—too long. My savage hunger rose inside me like a ravenous beast.

All I wanted was to feel something, and for some reason she made me feel things I had no right to feel. I'd visited every emotion with her from anger to laughter since we'd met. The only emotion left was regret, and I saw that coming at me fast the minute my hands traveled forward and grasped her breasts. Her nipples pebbled and strained under the lacy fabric of her bra.

A gentle moan of passion burst from her lips. "Oh God."

I pulled away for a second. I wanted inside her more than I wanted anything. Screwing her in the back seat of her Jeep was not my original intention, but the deep-seated ache I had needed to be relieved. Strong, vivid desire erased any sense of right or wrong.

"I want you," I whispered in her ear. "I want to be inside you now." I pumped my hips up against her body to show her what she'd done to me.

She pressed herself against my length and ground into me. "Yes, I want you, too." Her hands were on the zipper of my jacket, pulling it down tooth by tooth.

We were both completely caught up in the passion until a sharp rap on the window pulled us from our momentary bliss. The glow of a flashlight lit up the inside of the SUV, and a voice I recognized and loathed sliced through the air.

"This is Sheriff Stuart. I need you to exit the vehicle with your hands up."

My hands fell from her breasts as a growl fell from my mouth. "Asshole."

Ana shifted from my lap and righted her clothes. She opened her door first and stepped out of our warm cocoon into the frigid night air. I heard her feet hit the slick mud and watched as she slipped and fell on her ass, too fast for me to react.

The idiot didn't even try to help her. His attention was on me.

"Looky here. Isn't this interesting? Old man McKee said someone was driving too fast for conditions and crashed on his land. Get out of the car, boy."

I hated it when he called me "boy." He did it to piss me off because he was in a position of authority.

I raised my hands, because I didn't want to give him a reason to shoot me. He'd been looking for something to pin on me for years. I couldn't believe he'd finally found something. There was no way I could prove that I wasn't driving too fast for conditions.

I slid out and immediately went to help Ana up.

"Hands up, boy."

I raised my hands along with my voice. "Don't be an ass, Junior. Help the woman up."

He looked at Ana like he'd just realized she was there. She'd tried to right herself several times, but the mud was slippery, and she couldn't get a foothold.

Sheriff Stuart gripped her arm and pulled her roughly to a standing position. I moved forward. I didn't like the way he manhandled her. I backed off when his free hand went to his service weapon.

"I'll need your license."

Ana stepped between the sheriff and me. "You'll need my license. I was driving. Ryker was a passenger."

Sheriff Stuart eyed her with suspicion and then looked at me. "Is that true?"

I started to talk, but Ana interrupted. "I don't let people drive my Jeep, sir. I was driving. If you'll let me get my wallet from the front seat, I'd be happy to get you my license."

He looked her up and down like she was dessert. "What's your name, sweetheart?"

I wanted to punch his big, fat, bulbous nose. Now she was a sweetheart? Minutes ago, she wasn't worthy of a helping hand.

"I'm Ana Barrett. I just moved to Fury." Her voice was sweet. "I'm so glad you showed up."

He looked between Ana and me. "Is this piece of shit giving you a problem?" He flipped the snap on his holster like he was ready to draw.

"Oh, heavens, no. Ryker has been a saint." She smiled broadly, and I nearly sank to my knees into the mud. This woman was trying to save me. Didn't she know I was a lost cause? "My car started giving me problems at the fair. Nate took my pregnant friend home while Ryker offered to drive with me. We were going to take it to his shop so he could work on it, and then a silly cow crossed my path, and here I am."

I stood there straight-faced. She was lying to the law for me. Sure, we had talked about a tune-up, but there was no plan. At least there hadn't been, but I would make sure her Jeep ran like it was new. I rewarded loyalty, and this woman was putting it all on the line for me. Me, a man not worthy of her glance.

"I'd be negligent if I didn't warn you about him, Ana. Ryker Savage is not the type of man a beautiful young woman like yourself should be keeping company with."

She leaned against me. I wanted to wrap my arms around her in a show of solidarity, but I didn't dare move. Sheriff Stuart only needed me to flinch, and he'd find a reason to arrest me or shoot me.

"I thank you for your concern, but you needn't worry. Now, if you're going to write me a ticket, I'd like to get it over with, and then maybe you can help me get my car out of the mud."

I couldn't see her face, but she had to be smiling because the sheriff was speechless. I'd been dazzled by her smile more than once, so I almost felt sorry for the bastard. When he regained his gruff disposition, he demanded, "Why were you in the back seat?"

"It was warmer back there." She said it like it was common

sense, and he was an idiot. The truth was, he was an idiot, and I loved how easily she could put him off kilter.

The sheriff hooked his winch up to her back bumper and pulled the Jeep to the road.

Ana climbed into the front seat next to me where her feet didn't touch the gas pedal because of my adjustment. She looked over at the asshole standing next to her rolled down window. "Must have moved when we crashed." She adjusted the seat and turned the key. The engine sputtered and died. She pumped the gas and tried again. This time it turned over. With a wave of her hand, she said, "Thanks for your kindness, Sheriff." She pressed the gas, putting distance between the asshole and us.

When we were a safe distance away, I twisted in the seat and asked, "Why did you lie?"

She kept her eyes on the road and said, "I like you more than I like him. He seems like a jerk."

"You're a good judge of people."

She dropped one hand from the steering wheel and reached over the console to touch mine. "I hope so. You have a story to tell, Ryker, and I'm happy to listen when you're ready to talk."

I knew I'd tell her my story. She'd defended me, and in doing so she'd earned the right, but it wouldn't be tonight. I wasn't ready to ruin the best moment I'd had in years.

We rode the rest of the way into town holding hands. I gave her directions to my garage, and when she pulled into the driveway, I walked around to her side.

"Thanks for what you did. No one but Mona and Nate have ever stuck up for me." I leaned in and brushed my lips across hers. When I pulled away, she licked her lips like she was savoring the kiss.

"I have a feeling you're worth it." She rolled up her window and drove away.

Ana Barrett was changing my life from the top of my head to the tip of my toes and all the way back to my shriveled heart.

Chapter 19

ANA

A dark house meant Grace and Nate hadn't made it back from the diner. If Grace had been home, every light in the place would have been burning. She didn't like being alone. It was probably why she had so many companions.

The carnival-crash-kiss sequence had taken its toll on me, so I pulled out the extra blankets and pillow that Ryker had brought over and made a bed on the couch. I didn't have the heart to make a pregnant woman sleep on it, so it had become my new bed. I'd slept on worse. Hell, a few weeks ago I'd been sleeping on a pile of clothes in my room.

One look around the house, and I couldn't believe my eyes. It was a home. A real home with real furniture and walls the color of sunshine. I owed much of that to Ryker. Almost daily, he showed up with something that I lacked. Yesterday, it had been a lamp.

As soon as I pulled the tattered string, the soft glow of light filled the living room. Curled into the corner of the sofa with my computer in my lap, I Googled the town of Fury. Instead of looking at the town's webpage, I scrolled through the results until I came up with something that said *massacre*. There wasn't much listed, only that two rival gangs had gone to war and dozens of people had died. The deceased weren't listed.

Was this the incident that had molded Ryker into the man he was today? He'd been at my house more than his own over the past few weeks, but I knew nothing about him. All I knew was that he was handy and an excellent kisser.

I closed the browser and looked through my emails. The slew of new messages caused me to smile. I'd set up shop on Fiverr and offered to do any graphics work I could. Mostly, I was making logos for indie authors and fliers for garage sales, but every dollar counted, and through word of mouth, At Flight Graphics was getting business. Not the kind of business I'd dreamed of—I wasn't developing brochures for Fortune 500 companies—but I was making enough to pay my utilities and get a little extra work done on the house. For now, that was enough.

The door handle shook, and a moment later Grace walked in alone.

I slid my computer to the end table, another gift from Ryker.

"Where's Nate?" I didn't know where their night had taken them. Was it only the diner, or was it something more? Grace wasn't one to be cautious. That was obvious by her bouts of morning sickness and her tightening pants.

She hadn't decided what to do yet about her situation. She was burning up unpaid sick leave and hanging out with me until she had an epiphany.

"Hey, slut," she said to me as she walked in. Grace threw her purse on the floor in the corner and collapsed on the sofa next to me. In her hands was a white Styrofoam container.

"Slut?" I looked at her with a did-you-really-say-that look. "I'm not the one with the expanding waistline, my friend." There was no judgment in my voice; I loved Grace, and I'd be here for her no matter what. But if we were talking about sluts, Grace came closer to that description than I did. I could still count my sex partners on one hand. Maybe one hand and a finger from my other hand. In this day and age, that was almost virginal.

"I saw the way you two were looking at each other." She opened the box to reveal a huge slice of chocolate cake and two plastic forks.

I picked up a fork and shoved a bite into my mouth, hoping that she'd drop the subject if I were eating. "Mmm, this is good," I said with my mouth half full.

"Swallow and tell me everything." She pulled my blanket over her legs and forked a bite of cake. "Did you kiss him? God, I hope so. The tension around this place has been so tight."

I could feel the heat of my blush rise to my cheeks. Was the glow of the light too dim for her to notice? I prayed so.

I got my answer when I looked up and saw her wide grin. "Did you have sex with him?" She looked down at my makeshift bed and swiftly stood. She turned around like a dog chasing its tail and looked over her shoulder toward her butt. "Ew, did I get anything on my pants?"

I picked up the pillow and swatted at her, almost knocking the cake from her hands. That would have been a crime, because the cake was amazing.

"No, I didn't sleep with him. We rode the rides and came home."

Grace narrowed her eyes at me. We'd been friends since I could remember, and it was hard to get anything past her. She was like a walking lie detector.

"I want to hear it all." She licked a bit of chocolate frosting from her lip and settled back onto the couch.

I told her about the rides and the maze of mirrors. I told her how we'd crashed and about the asshole sheriff.

"What about the kiss?" She leaned forward like she was watching a movie and the good part was about to start.

I sat back and closed my eyes, reliving the kisses we'd shared in the back seat of my Jeep. "He's an excellent kisser."

She reached over and pulled my hair. It was such a childish thing to do. "That's all you got for me?"

"What do you want me to say? He tasted like funnel cake and sex? He made my lady parts quiver and hunger for more? He made me forget my life was shit for a second?"

She rolled her body back a bit. Enough to take a good look at me. "Is all of that true?"

I couldn't lie to her. I wouldn't lie to her. "Yes, every single word is true."

She closed the box, leaned forward, and hugged me. "Looks like you found your hawk."

I touched my hand to my lips. They still tingled from his kiss. "Maybe I have, but what about you? Are you making a move on Nate?"

She shook her head hard enough to jumble brain cells. "No way. I mean, I like him, but I'm trying out something new."

"Oh yeah, what's that?"

"Men as friends. It's a concept I'd never considered, but it's amazing what you can learn about a man when he isn't buried inside of you groaning."

"Do tell." I pulled the corner of the blanket up to my chin.

"I can't explain it, but he's different from most guys I meet."

Grace wasn't speaking like she normally did when the topic was men. The way she talked about Nate was different. There was no lift of the brow, purr of her voice, or lick of her lip. She was building her first friendship with a man. My friend was growing up, and it was about time because soon she'd be raising a child of her own, and she wouldn't be able to do that and act like a child herself.

"He's different because he's not a rooster." Nate was handsome for sure, but he wasn't a pretty boy—preppy, maybe, but in no way pretty. "What will you do with a man you aren't having sex with?"

She giggled and covered her mouth with her hand. "I am so out of my element." She raised her head and looked at me. "What will you do with a man you'll be having sex with?" Her hands went to her stomach.

"I'll enjoy every inch of him." I thought about the giant of a man and knew he was big everywhere. "Isn't it time I enjoyed something?"

Grace covered a yawn and rose from the couch. "I think you should let me sleep here." She fluffed the pillow where I would lay my head.

"Nonsense. I'm happy to let my pregnant friend sleep in my bed. By the way—" I looked at her stomach, "—have you decided what you're going to do?"

"I've decided to keep the baby. The rest I'll figure out along the way." Her expression wasn't one of a happy pregnant woman, but one of a woman confused, yet I had faith in Grace. She was strong, and she'd come out of this okay. "Thanks for everything, Ana."

I looked around the house and smiled. "Isn't it amazing that out of my anguish we have a place of sanctuary on a street called Abundant in a town called Fury?"

"Imagine that," she said before she disappeared down the hallway.

I pulled my computer back into my lap and worked on a new logo. This one was for a horror writer who wanted his name drawn in blood. While I tried to get the drip right, I heard a noise on the side of the house. A peek out the window showed the shadow of a man. I hunkered down and peeked over the arm of the sofa. The glow of a cigarette ember lit the dark night. Something was familiar about him. His height and breadth could only be one man—Ryker. I relaxed, ran my fingers through my hair, and straightened his flannel shirt over my body. I hadn't taken it off because it was comfortable. It felt right.

My feet wanted to run to him, but my mind told me to walk slowly. To race to him would give him too much power, and giving Ryker the upper hand wouldn't be wise. He was short-tempered and moody and used to living by his own rules. Grace was right; my hawk was a predator, and if not approached with care, he could pick my bones clean.

I opened the door and stepped onto the porch. A soft wind swirled around me, bringing the scent of him. That was Ryker, clean and fresh and strong. A tinge of smoke wafted in on the breeze, and I scrunched my nose. That wasn't Ryker, or at least I didn't think it was. "You smoke?"

He pushed off the trunk of the enormous oak tree and tossed his cigarette to the ground, smashing it with the toe of his boot. Out of the shadows, he stepped in front of me. "Generally, no. But when I'm stressed, yes." He dropped his head as if shamed.

I don't know what compelled me to touch him, but I couldn't resist laying my hand on his chest. I felt his heart thumping under my fingertips. "What stresses you?"

"Everything stresses me. Sheriff Stuart. This damn house. This damn town. It all stresses me the hell out." He kicked at the dead grass under his boot. "You stress me out."

"Me?" I gripped the edge of his jacket. "Me? Why?"

His gaze lasered into me. "When you dropped me off, I went upstairs and tried to sleep, but I couldn't. I'm fighting with myself." He reached for my cheek. His fingers sure and able. His touch soft. "I want you." He threaded his hand through my hair. "I know if I have you, I'll destroy you. I destroy everything I touch."

He leaned closer and then stepped back but didn't drop his gaze. Didn't drop his hold.

I leaned in. I wanted him closer. I wanted the kiss he was denying me.

"Screw it, I'm weak when it comes to you." He pulled me into his arms, and his lips crushed mine with a ferocity I'd never experienced. I tried to throttle back the dizzying current that raced through me, but it was no use. If Ryker was intent on destroying me, I was a willing victim.

Chapter 20

RYKER

The smart thing would have been to leave, because if I didn't leave, her life would change, and I wasn't sure if it was for the better. I pulled back and looked into her eyes. They were heavy with desire.

As if our lips were magnets, she pulled me in again. My tongue traced the soft fullness of her mouth and slipped inside to take more. I kissed her like she was the last thing I'd taste before I die, and if she was, I'd be satisfied.

She shuddered in my embrace. Was it from the cold or the kiss? When I wrapped my arms tightly around her, I didn't care. All I wanted was more. She was like getting a taste of my favorite ice cream. A taste wasn't enough, and I knew if I didn't stop now, I'd devour her.

I warred within myself. Keep her. Let her go. With reluctance, I pulled away. "I'm sorry. I shouldn't have come here." I scrubbed my fingers through my hair and turned to leave.

She grabbed my arm and tugged me to the front door. "Stay," she pleaded. "Please."

I looked past her to the door. It was such a tempting offer.

Should I say yes? Could I say no?

"It's late." I pulled my arm from hers and tucked my hands in my front pockets. I lowered my head, because if I saw what I heard in her voice reflected in her eyes, I wouldn't be able to leave.

"I'm up. You're up. Let's be up together."

I made the mistake of looking up and seeing her eyes. The last time I'd seen anything resembling that was when my mom had stood at the Christmas pageant and watched me play St. Nick. She'd mouthed the lines I couldn't remember the day before and that I'd hoped I wouldn't forget that night. I had recited them with perfection, and I had been rewarded with my favorite ice cream after the play.

Oh, screw it. I stomped up the steps and opened the door for both of us. Inside, the soft yellow glow of the lamp threw shadows against the yellow walls. Everything in here was familiar, and yet it wasn't. Ana had a way of taking shit and making it shine. Even Dad's old desk was new again. Painted in cream and soft green with vines twining up the legs, it resembled something you'd find in a high-end store, not something that was recycled from a garage.

"I like everything you've done here." I walked around the room and traced the edges of the furniture with my fingertips. The couch and tables never looked this good in my place. The old leather chair looked like a loved piece of furniture with its throw pillow positioned just right. At my place, it looked like an old leather chair ready for the junkyard.

Nate called Ana Ms. Sunshine, and in a way, she was exactly that: everything she cast her light on seemed brighter and happier. I closed my eyes and said a silent prayer that I wouldn't dim her in any way.

"You want a glass of wine?" she asked sweetly.

"Sure, I can get it if you tell me where."

"It's the cheap box wine. I can't afford the good stuff, and honestly, I'm not sure I like the good stuff." She walked to the kitchen, and I followed. She opened the refrigerator and pulled out the box of Gallo Chablis. "Grab two glasses." Her finger pointed the way, and I found two mason jars on the bottom shelf. She still didn't have much, but for a girl who'd shown up with only clothes, a lawn chair, and a popped air mattress, I'd say she was doing all right.

A feeling of goodness filled my chest, because I knew I'd brought something of value to her life, even if it was only hand-me-downs.

She pushed in the spigot and filled the jars half full before putting the box back on the top shelf.

"Where's Grace?" I assumed she and Nate had made it back from the diner.

Ana walked from the kitchen and nodded toward the hallway. "She's sleeping. It's been a tough week for her."

"Who's the father?" Grace didn't look pregnant yet, so she couldn't be that far along, but the words *baby* and *prenatal* got tossed around a lot—it didn't take a rocket scientist to understand what was going on.

"Her boss."

I swallowed a drink of wine. "Shit. That's not good. Is it?"

She plopped down on the couch that was made up into a bed and patted the spot beside her. All the fight I had in me had gone the moment I walked into the house. In truth, all the fight had left the minute she'd climbed into the back seat with me.

"No, it's not good. He told her to get rid of it, but she won't. That's not Grace. She can overlook twelve years of Catholic school when it comes to premarital sex and birth control, but there's no way she'd terminate her pregnancy."

"What an asshole. I hate everyone who doesn't see the value of a child." I clenched my jaw, trying not to say more. I'd been in many homes that saw children as a commodity—a paycheck. *The more, the better* was their motto. They collected orphans like rare coins, but instead of shining them and keeping them safe, they tarnished them and then made them feel worthless with their words and their fists.

I hadn't realized I'd fisted up my free hand until Ana covered it with hers. "Tell me about you."

"There's nothing I could say that would impress you."

Her smile was disarming. "I'm not asking you to impress me. I'm asking you to trust me and talk to me."

It was like she could look inside my soul and see the wounds that were still bleeding.

"What do you want to know?" I leaned back on the couch and let my arm hang across the back cushions. My fingers found her hair and began to twirl it around and around.

"Let's start with why you needed to work for me." She moved closer until she was next to me. The sides of our bodies pressed together like peanut butter and jelly.

"I've got two brothers, but one has been missing since we were put in foster care. Private investigators are expensive."

"Oh my God, that's awful. No one can tell you where he was placed?" Her hand fell to my thigh and drew a zigzag pattern up and down the faded denim.

"Nope, the adoption was closed. Silas and I have no idea where he is, but we know our parents would have wanted us to be together."

"Where's Silas?" She went from drawing with one finger to rubbing my thigh with her palm. The way her hand caressed me made me hard.

"He's in Afghanistan. Army. I'm hoping he comes home soon. I'm always hoping." I twisted halfway around to face her.

"He's the one you went to jail for, right?"

"Yep, and I'd do it again."

"How did your parents die?" She stiffened when she asked it, or maybe it was me who turned to steel.

The subject always caused my hackles to rise. "Listen, I don't want to talk about it, but I'll give you the shortened version. There was a major gun battle here twenty years ago. A lot of bullets flew, and a lot of people died, including the people that used to live here. Many kids were orphaned that day, not only Silas, Decker, and me. It was a tragedy that could have been avoided."

She curled into me. "Thanks for letting me in."

I pulled her into my lap and crushed my mouth to hers. She took every punishing kiss like she needed them as much as I did. Our lips were glued together as her fingers worked the zipper of my hoodie. I shrugged it off and broke the kiss just long enough to pull my T-shirt over my head.

The flannel she wore was gone in seconds, and my hands were on her breasts. The air around us crackled with need. I needed. She needed. There was a hunger that floated around us. A hunger that had to be fed. In one movement, I switched her position from on top of me to under me.

I unclasped her bra and tossed it aside. Dusky pink nipples pebbled against her milky white skin. I pulled back, looking for any sign that she wanted me to stop, but her eyes said *more*, and her hands tugging at the button of my jeans sealed the deal.

While I stood to remove my pants, she shimmied out of hers and lay naked on the sheet before me. I was no stranger to women, but this one was special all the way from her pink painted toenails to the puckered scar under her collarbone.

I traced it with my fingers, but she pushed me away as if it caused her pain. I knew the pain of scars that showed and those that didn't. I stared into her brown eyes and tried to let her know that I understood.

"Are you sure?" I asked, poised above her. I didn't know what I'd do if she denied me.

"I'm not sure about anything, but I'm not turning back. I want this. I want you." Her voice had gone from sweet to needy. The gravelly tone sent a quiver to my groin, and my balls tightened painfully.

I pulled a condom from my pocket and slid it onto my length. I loved the way her eyes grew large as the rubber sheathed me inch by inch. I looked down at her with awe. She was beautiful. A tiny thing with a big attitude and great breasts.

I fell to my knees in front of her and pulled one tight nipple into my mouth while I rolled the other between two fingertips. I wanted to tease her forever, but it had been too long since I'd sunk myself into a woman. Ana's moans of pleasure spurred me on, and I moved lower to taste her. When her legs fell open, I gazed at her glistening flesh and growled. But it was when I dipped my tongue into her heat and pulled her taste into my mouth that I became lost.

I feasted on her until her hands gripped my hair and she shook under my mouth.

"Oh God," she repeated over and over until her hips bucked, and then I pulled her tight bundle of nerves between my lips and sucked. She stilled for a second, and then her body exploded beneath me. I didn't stop until she begged for it. That was a beautiful sound, Ana begging me to stop. Nirvana would be reached when she begged me to start again.

I'd thought that I'd be able to sleep with her and forget her, get her out of my system. And maybe that could happen, but something told me that Ana Barrett was going to be an addiction I couldn't kick.

One of my legs was bent next to her on the couch, and the other was on the ground. Ana's legs were wrapped around my hips. My steely rod danced at her entrance.

I pressed inside. The tip was in, and it was nearly enough to send me over the edge. She looked up at me with passion-heavy eyes and licked her lips. Lips I wanted wrapped around my erection one day.

Her fingers traced the bird on my chest, then lowered to my hips. She grabbed them and pulled me forward. I filled her inch-by-inch. Her body tensed at the intrusion.

"Let me in." I lowered my lips to hers and kissed her softly while I plunged the rest of the way inside her. I ate up her groan and waited until she relaxed around me.

"God, you're massive," she whispered against my lips.

"God, you're tight." I pulled out and slid in and started a rhythm that she met stroke for stroke.

The couch wasn't the ideal place for a first sexual encounter. We screwed like teenagers in their parents' living room. Anytime I got too loud, she pulled me down and kissed me. "I don't want to wake Grace," she whispered.

I didn't give a damn about Grace, but for some reason I did care about Ana, and so I pulled in my voice and bit my lips each time I wanted to moan or groan. The pace increased, and her head snapped from side to side.

"I'm close again." She lifted her hips and pounded upward. I adjusted my angle, hoping to hit the perfect spot to take her over the edge. The flutter of her muscles started weak but soon became like a throbbing vise around me, and there was no turning back. She stilled as the waves of pleasure silently washed over her. I stilled as my release broke free. What I experienced in that moment scared the shit out of me. A feeling of peace blanketed me, and I wanted to live inside Ana forever. I'd never known anything that good.

We lay there for a minute until my body became too heavy for her to bear. I was almost standing when she pulled me back for a kiss. "I don't regret that. I hope you don't either." The softness in her eyes tugged at the space in my chest where my heart used to reside. Was it possible that Ana had planted a seed of hope that could bloom into something more?

"I won't regret that either. It was amazing." I covered her with the blanket and found my way to the bathroom, where I disposed of the condom. When I looked into the mirror, I saw a man I didn't recognize. The man in the mirror wasn't full of anger. The man staring back at me was full of calm.

When I returned to the living room, Ana was dressed and lying on the couch. This time, she wasn't wearing my flannel. She was wearing my T-shirt. She pulled it to her nose and inhaled, and that space in my chest filled.

"Do you want me to stay or go?" I had no idea why I even asked. I knew I needed to go before things went too far. Staying here would only make things worse. I didn't do attachments. I didn't need complications. My life was a shit storm, and I didn't want to bring anyone else into the eye of the disaster.

"No, stay with me for a while." She scooted as far back into the couch cushions as possible, making as much room for me as she could. I pulled on my jeans and went to her. I was a big man and took up the whole couch and then some. So instead of crushing her into the corner, I picked her up and laid her on my body. Her cheek rested on my chest, cradled perfectly by my hawk's wings.

I rubbed my hands up and down her back. "Where did you get that scar?" It was an odd scar, much like my own, only there was no exit wound.

Her fingers reached up to trace mine. "I was in a car accident when I was little. A truck lost its load of rebar, and my family suffered the disaster. My parents died instantly. I was lucky, I guess because it only went through one side of me."

I squeezed my hands against her, pulling her tighter into my chest. I knew the pain of losing parents. "I'm sorry for your loss."

She reached up and pulled the blanket from the back of the couch over both of us. "Weird that we were both orphaned so young."

Nothing surprised me anymore. "Yeah, Nate was telling me about some article that said orphans struggled with relationships. Guess that's why I'm twenty-eight and still single."

"You, too? Grace told me about that same study." Ana wormed her body around until she was comfortable. "Weird." A few minutes later, her breath became slow and shallow. I held her for several hours before I slipped out from under her and quietly made my way to the door. I took one last look over my shoulder at the woman who made me feel something other than rage, and I knew I was in deep shit.

Chapter 21

ANA

The smell of coffee and bacon wafted through the morning air. No longer was I splayed across Ryker's chest. Though he was gone, the tenderness between my legs confirmed to me that he'd been here. I rolled myself into a sitting position and stretched. My eyes burned from leaving my contacts in too long. I was trying to squeeze another week out of them, but if it resulted in pain, it wasn't worth it.

Grace appeared in the kitchen door. "I want details."

I dropped my face into my hands and pretended to rub the sleep out of my eyes, but in reality, I was trying to hide the blush that I knew colored my face. I should have known Grace would somehow know, but I looked around, trying to figure out how.

It was like she'd read my mind. "Two half glasses of wine, and you're wearing his T-shirt." She prodded me with a plate full of bacon and eggs and sat down beside me. "Spill."

"I don't kiss and tell."

"That's bullshit. You gave me every last detail about Mark Hopkins', and he wasn't even interesting." She nibbled on the edge of the bacon and waited expectantly. "At least tell me he made you come."

My head spun toward her. She was relentless, and I knew if I didn't give her something, she'd make it the topic of discussion for the entire day.

"Twice." My stomach knotted with yummy tension at the thought of what he'd done to me. There was no romance or finesse; it was pure carnal sex—and it was amazing.

"Holy shit." She took a bite of her overcooked scrambled eggs and sighed. "I'm going to miss orgasms."

"It's not like your vagina is closed down forever."

"No? Have you ever Googled stretch marks? What about vaginal delivery? If eight pounds can squeeze itself out of there, how will it ever feel the same? The next time I have sex, I'm probably going to have to tie a lifeline around the guy's waist to pull him out, or maybe attach a two-by-four to his ass so he doesn't fall in."

"Oh, please. First of all, most guys don't care about stretch marks. The minute a woman drops her top, all they see are boobs. Nothing else matters. Second, if vaginas didn't bounce back, no one would have siblings."

"You do remember that we are both only children, right?" She used her bacon like a spoon and scooped up a bite of egg.

"I'm an only child because my parents died. You're an only child because your dad is a jerk."

It was true. During her mom's only pregnancy, Grace's father had had an affair. Her mother didn't let him back into her bed after that. Mrs. Faraday turned to wine and travel, and Mr. Faraday turned away from his mistress and turned toward God. He went to seminary school and became a deacon. Their family became the model of Christianity to the outside world. The only problem was that Grace was more like Mary Magdalene than the Virgin Mary.

"I'm not convinced that what you say is true."

"Look at the bright side. You won't need that boob job after all."

"There is that." Grace set down her plate and cupped her already heavy breasts. "So are you and Ryker a thing now? Didn't you tell me his name was Hawk?"

"I did, but apparently it's a nickname only used by his inner circle."

Grace scrunched up her face. "He has one friend. That's a damn small circle." She licked her fingers and pressed them against the bacon crumbs on her plate. "And doesn't climbing between your legs last night give you access to that circle?"

Grace's reasoning was twisted, but her question was valid. What did last night change for Ryker and me? "I'm not going to make too much of last night. It was nice, and I learned a lot about the man."

My friend shook her head. "You always liked the ones with the broken wings."

"Call me crazy, but I'm a magnet for tall, brooding, wounded men—the more broken the better." Gramps had said I had a savior complex; Grams had once said I was like my mom, always falling for the wrong kind of man. In her mind, I was a bum magnet, and she might have been right. Ryker was plenty extreme; he was angry and hurt and fractured. But something inside told me he was worth my effort, and I wasn't one to give up easily. Hell, I'd lived in an apartment with a blowup mattress and a plastic lawn chair for six months. If that wasn't a testament to my will to prevail, I didn't know what was.

"Be careful, or you'll end up like me."

I stared at my beautiful friend and brushed her red hair from her face. "I could only be so lucky to be as amazing as you."

A tear slipped from her eye. "Now you're making me cry. What kind of friend are you?"

Pregnancy was doing a real number on her emotions. One minute she'd laugh, and the next she'd cry. It was a roller coaster, but I'd take that ride with her because Grace was all that I had, and I loved her. "I'm the keeping kind."

She leaned in and hugged me tightly. "I don't want to be a burden, but can I stay longer?"

"Let's find another bed, and you can stay forever." I rubbed her back and held her like Grams would hold me when my life seemed to be falling apart. Back then, it had been because someone had teased me or stolen the boy I had a crush on. Grace's issues were a lot bigger and would require more hugs.

She sat up and looked at me. "Really?"

"Of course, but there are conditions." I picked up our plates and walked them into the kitchen. She followed behind.

"What are the terms?"

"You provide the chocolate cake once a week, and the rest we'll figure out."

She leaned against the counter while I soaped up the sponge. "How about I buy a new bed for the spare room and take you out for dinner and chocolate cake once a week?" She bounced forward with another carrot to dangle in front of me, even though I'd already told her she could stay forever. That was Grace. She always gave more than required. "Oh, and I get a television and cable so we can watch reruns of *Friends*."

"You drive a hard bargain, but I think those are good terms." We gave each other one last hug, and she ran toward the bedroom, mumbling off items on her to-do list: "Get a bed. Get cake. Cut my boss' nut sack off."

I hoped she was successful with her first two goals. The final one, not so much; visiting her in jail would be tough.

I'd finished washing and drying the plates when a knock sounded at the door. I rushed to it, thinking it was Ryker, but I was greeted by Mona and a pitcher of lemonade. She'd been coming over a couple times a week. Her favorite thing was razzing Grace. They were quite a pair. One was a young woman who loved to talk about sex, and the other an old lady who never tired of listening.

"Hey, Mona, come on in." I opened the door wide and waited for her to enter. "Grace is getting dressed so she can regale you with stories about long nights of hot sex." I took the lemonade from her and led her to the leather chair. It was her favorite place to sit.

"I'm not here for Grace's story. I want to know about you and Ryker. Was it as amazing as I would imagine? Can he bring the goods?"

I rolled my eyes and groaned. "You are not blind. You have an eagle's eye behind those dark glasses."

"The Lord blesses me with moments of clarity. Last night, I had terrible gas that kept me up, and so I sat on the porch and sipped tea. I watched that boy sneak out of your house in the wee hours. Only one thing happens in the wee hours." She pointed to the lemonade and Solo cups, and I poured us both a glass.

"You're wrong, Mona, two things happen in the wee hours. Apparently, men sneak out of my house and you get gas." I left it at that, despite her sly hints for more juicy details.

A few minutes later, Grace came into the living room and invited Mona to go shopping with her, and I was never so grateful to be alone. I looked at my bare walls and decided that today would be art day, and I'd start with the picture I painted for Grams. It was the last thing she responded to, so obviously it was important to her, and that made me feel good. Grams' picture would have a place of honor in the home she gifted me. I'd hang it so everyone would see it when they walked in.

Once the picture was up, the rest of the walls looked barren, so I grabbed my craft paints and started painting a border of brambles and branches up near the ceiling. Every so often, I'd add a bird. I'd placed a finch in the brambles, and a blue jay on the tip of a branch with a little sparrow tucked under his wing. I'd wound my way around one wall and had started on the next when a knock sounded at the door. I climbed down the ladder to see who was there.

In front of me was Ryker. His eyes were no longer hard and angry but soft and inviting. Their blue was like the summer sky.

"Hey, I wasn't sure if you were going to come around today."

"Why wouldn't I?" He moved forward and brushed his lips against mine. "There's no place I'd rather be."

My insides twirled and flipped. He made me feel emotions I'd never allowed myself to explore. Things like love and happiness and hope. I leaned against the doorjamb. "I didn't know what to expect."

"I would have come earlier, but I had someone interested in buying a motorcycle I'm selling."

I wondered whether things were that bad for him. I knew he needed money, but selling his motorcycle seemed like a big deal. "You sure you want to sell it?"

"I don't, but it's a necessity. I need to pay for the investigator." At the mention of the investigator, the light in his eyes dimmed to a cloudy gray. "Are you going to invite me in?"

I swung open the door, and he stepped aside. His eyes went directly to the painting on the wall and then followed my hand-painted border around the room.

He marched to Grams' painting and took it off the wall. I expected him to pull it closer to look at the detail, but he didn't. He threw it across the room and turned on me. "What the hell are you pulling here?"

I stumbled back until I hit the wall. "I'm not pulling anything here, and why would you do that?" I shot forward to where the picture hit the wall and fell behind the couch. When I picked it up, I started to cry, because the frame was broken and a small tear marred the canvas. "How could you do that? This was one of the few things I had left of my Grams." I pulled the broken picture to my chest.

"How could I? How could you? You knew this house was special to me." His eyes went to the lines on the doorframe that I hadn't had the heart to paint over. "You knew she was special to me." He fisted his hands and pounded them against his thighs.

"I don't know what the hell you're talking about. I rarely know what you're talking about, because you don't share much of anything. Last night was the first time you really talked to me. I thought we were making progress."

Ryker stomped toward the door. "Last night was a mistake." He brushed past Grace and Mona, who were walking up the sidewalk. He didn't say a word to them before he hopped into his car and sped off.

"What the hell happened in here?" Grace helped Mona over the threshold and looked around the room. "You've been painting."

I set the broken picture on the floor and slid down the wall. "Apparently, Ryker isn't a fan of birds."

Mona walked to where I'd placed the picture. She picked it up and brought it close to her face. "He likes birds all right. It's just this bird was special, and he feels responsible for her death."

We all sat down while Mona filled in the blanks of Ryker's life. She told us about Sparrow, her mother, Finch, and her father, Jay, whom many called Blue because of the color of his eyes. She talked about the War Birds and their hangout, called The Nest. She retold the horrors of that day and how Ryker blamed himself for everything.

At that, Grace chimed in. "It sounds like it was the girl's fault. If she hadn't followed Ryker, the box wouldn't have tumbled over, and everyone would still be alive."

"How can you blame a four-year-old, Grace? Imagine your child making a mistake and being memorialized as the blame of some horrific accident." I didn't know why I fought to protect the little girl. I didn't know her, but I knew that at her age, she wasn't capable of knowing her actions could create such havoc. "If anyone is to blame, it's the parents. Who brings their kids up in a gang? Who asks an eight-year-old boy to babysit three children?" My heart broke for Ryker. I was angry that he'd damaged my picture, but I was more upset because I hadn't had all the facts. And now that I did, I was heartbroken for the man who'd lost and given so much.

Mona raised her hands in question. "Would have, should have, could have, it's all speculation, but I agree with you, Ana. Ryker isn't at fault, and yet he's been carrying the blame on his shoulders for two decades."

I stood up and grabbed my purse from the floor in the corner.

"Where are you going?" Grace asked.

"I'm going to bandage a broken wing."

Chapter 22

RYKER

When I left Ana's house, I had nowhere to run to but Nate's. I found him in the paint department, tossing expired cans into a cart.

He glanced up and said, "Perfect timing. I'm clearing out the expired exterior paint. It's not actually bad. It's just past its prime. I thought I'd bring it over to Ana's, and maybe you can help her paint the outside of the house."

"I'm not helping her do another damn thing." I crossed my arms and leaned heavily against a paintbrush display, making several brushes fall from their hooks to the floor.

"Whoa, man, what happened?" Nate bent over and picked up the brushes. "Last night I thought I'd never seen you so happy, and now look at you. She wouldn't put out?" He raised his eyes in question.

"Screw you." Maybe coming here had been a mistake. Nate was my best friend—hell, my only friend—but he could never understand. He hadn't lost what I'd lost.

"No, screw her, not me. You're not my type." He pushed me to the side to rehang what fell to the floor. "I thought for sure you two hit it off. I even kept Grace out long enough so you could get a quickie."

"It wasn't quick, you asshole."

His laugh echoed through the aisle. "Good man. So you got laid. I would figure that would put a smile on your face for at least a day or so. That bad, huh?"

I wanted to punch the bastard in his face for talking about Ana in that way. "You're an asshole. Last night was a perfect moment in my less than perfect life."

He went back to stacking cans into the basket. "If she's so damn perfect, then what the hell is the problem?"

I rubbed my jaw, trying to calm the ache caused from constant clenching. "She hung a picture of a sparrow in her house."

"And that's a crime?"

"It was a sparrow, Nate. What the hell?"

Nate's father walked out of the back office. "Take that language outside."

"Sure thing, Dad." Nate pushed me toward the door. "Get a grip on yourself. It's a picture of a bird. Lots of people like birds."

"She hung a picture of a sparrow in Sparrow's house!" I yelled, pulling at my hair.

"How the hell is she supposed to know what that means? You're going to give up the best thing you've had in years because the woman likes birds? I've always looked up to you. You've been bigger than life in my eyes. You've walked through fire and came out alive, and you're going to let a picture of a sparrow clip the wings of a hawk?" Nate shook his head and walked away, leaving me alone in the parking lot.

When I got back to the garage, Ana was waiting there, leaning against her Jeep. She pushed off and stood tall as my car neared hers. All the way home, I thought of Nate's words. It was a picture of a bird; fate had been a cruel bastard to make it a sparrow. He was right; it couldn't be her fault since she didn't know. I hadn't fully shared that part of me because I was too ashamed and too afraid that she'd see me like everyone else did.

I parked my car and walked toward her. The words *I'm sorry* were on my lips, but she beat me to them.

"I'm so sorry, Ryker. I had no idea. Mona explained it all."

I stood in front of her and cupped her cheek. "*You're* sorry? I acted like a deranged fool, and the thing is, I hated Sparrow more than I liked her. She was a sassy thing that was always under my feet. It's funny how time can change your perception. How you can dislike someone and then turn them into a saint the minute they die. I'm pretty sure if she was around today, I wouldn't like her much. I'd hate her for following me into the garage, and I'd blame her for everyone's death. The same way everyone has blamed me for years." I lifted her into my arms and carried her toward the garage. "I'm sorry. I'm so sorry, Ana." I kicked the tools aside that littered my path and rushed to the stairs that led to my room. "Forgive me for being such a—"

She pressed a finger to my lips. "Forgive you for caring so much about a little girl? Of course. I'd forgive you for anything, Ryker. You're a good man."

I gripped her ass tighter and raced up the stairs two at a time. "I'm not good, and I don't deserve you."

"You are good, and I'm your reward." She tugged and pulled at my shirt until it bunched under my armpits. She traced the lines of my tattoo and followed the right wing all the way to the end where it covered a tiny sparrow. "Even after her death, you protected her and put her under your wing, but who protects you?" She peppered my chest with kisses, and I walked down the hallway to my bedroom and laid her on my unmade bed.

I shed the shirt and went to work on her clothes while she tugged at the button of my jeans, and like last night, we were naked in seconds. "Why me?" I asked her as I trailed kisses down her body.

"Why not you?" Her hands explored me like she was memorizing every hill and valley. Her fingers pressed gently against my scar, but it didn't pain me to have them there. The heat of healing spread through my body and wrapped like a fiery rope around my heart.

Sparrow might have shriveled one organ—my heart—but Ana was making it swell again, along with my passion. Maybe hope wasn't such a dangerous thing after all.

I positioned myself above her. "I'll try to be worthy of you."

"I'll make you rise to the occasion." She reached down and gripped my shaft. "Oh look, you already have."

Without hesitation, I plunged inside of her. My body stilled while her heat enveloped me, pulling me in until I was fully rooted. Ana was the only safe place for me. "God, you feel amazing."

She wrapped her legs around my waist and pressed herself against me. "So good," she moaned.

Last night was all about sex, but today I'd make it about something else. Today, it would be about her and the place she was taking inside my heart.

"I want to please you." My hips moved slowly back and forth. It was torture. Pure. Beautiful. Torture. I plunged in and out of her slick heat. Her breath quickened, and a sheen of sweat built on her brow. Ana wasn't the kind of woman who only took. She matched me stroke by stroke, giving right back to me.

"If you pleased me any more, I might not ever leave this bed." She rose up and sucked on my nipple, which sent a jolt of electricity straight down to my groin. I gripped her hands and held them down, trying to stave off the orgasm that was teetering on the edge. "Stop, or I'll cum."

She fought my hold but quickly gave up when she realized I wasn't going to release or relent. I closed my eyes and willed the pulsing to stop.

"Isn't coming the objective?"

"Generally, yes, but I'm not wrapped."

It took her a minute to process what I was saying. "Shit, Ryker." She pushed against my chest.

"Babe, I'm on the edge, don't move." The first hot rush shot forward, and I pulled out in time to watch ropes squirt across her stomach. "God, I'm sorry, it's that you felt so damn good."

"Oh my God. What were you thinking?" She looked down at her stomach and then relaxed. "It's a good thing you're fast, because I'm not on birth control."

I collapsed beside her. "Fast isn't a rumor I want passed around." I reached for my discarded T-shirt and cleaned my mess from her stomach. "I'm so sorry."

"We're good." Her brow furrowed until I started kissing her again.

I had a pretty short recovery time. By the time I kissed my way down her body, I was as hard as a rock again. This time, I leaned over and pulled a strip of condoms from my drawer.

"Feeling pretty confident, aren't you?" She pulled the string of five from my hand. While she separated the perforated edges, I nipped and nibbled my way down her stomach.

"Do you doubt my ability to deliver?" I shimmied down to the space between her legs. Neatly trimmed hair formed a triangle, much like an arrow guiding me in the direction where pure pleasure waited. I gripped her thighs and spread her wide open. It was a damn beautiful sight to see her pink and swollen from me.

"I don't doubt—" Any further words were silenced by the heat of my tongue. Hours could be spent lapping up her sweetness. Days hearing her moans of pleasure. Years feeling her quiver under my lips. Decades spent listening to her scream my name. She was a lifetime of pure bliss.

After the second orgasm, she begged for more, and although I loved the sound of her words wanting me so desperately, I had needs of my own that required her hot, wet glove. I pulled her legs to my shoulders and buried myself balls deep inside her.

What started slow built to a frenzied pace. Our bodies, drenched in sweat, slapped together until we were both spent and satisfied. I curled around her body and held her close. My world was perfect.

"What am I going to do with you?" I whispered against her ear.

"Love me," she whispered back.

The idea sent my spirits soaring. Could it be possible for me to love and not lose?

Her body was soft and warm beside me. My mind was clear, and my heart was full. I was already in love. She didn't have to ask; it was a given. What I'd thought was hate this morning when I saw the picture of a sparrow was simply fate's reminder that I had to let the other go in order to open my heart completely to Ana. From this day forward, I would bury the past and look toward a future with this woman.

But on the tail of bliss was fear, and it raced through my blood. To love her was to risk everything. To not love her was to have nothing. There was no choice.

Chapter 23

ANA

I woke to a darkened room and the sound of water in the distance. The bed beside me still held the heat of his body. My thighs were bruised from his power. My heart sang with the song of his love.

Life turned on a dime. Only weeks ago I was an orphan and alone, and tonight I lay in the arms of a man who twisted my heart at every glance and sent butterflies aflutter in my stomach.

A dry mouth pulled me from the warm cocoon of Ryker's bed and the scent of him on the sheets. His fresh T-shirt lay on the end of the mattress, waiting for him, but he was too late. I slid it over my head and let it fall off one shoulder. I padded barefoot down the hallway into the living room and flipped on the light switch. The room was empty except for an old leather chair in the center that matched mine. The hardwood floor was clean but faded around darker areas where furniture used to sit. The furniture that now filled my home. I stepped on every dark area and matched the shape with what was in my house. I hopped from where the couch sat, to where the chair sat, to where the side table sat. It brought me to a wall of photos.

Three boys. The end picture was a baby with big blue eyes. Next in line was a smaller version of Ryker. The third picture was Ryker. He still had the same smile despite the fact that he rarely used it. But when he did, the world was brighter. Next in line were what I assumed were his parents. Mona said Ryker's dad's name was Raptor, which was fitting for the leader of a motorcycle gang called the War Birds. His mother, Dove, stood next to his father. Her blonde hair fell in deep contrast to their father's dark.

A ringtone broke the silence, and I ran toward the sound. Ryker's computer sat on the counter lit up with an incoming call from Silas. I wasn't sure whether I should answer or ignore it. When it got to the fourth ring, I pressed the button that said *answer with video*. A man in a green T-shirt and camouflage cap sat dead center on the screen. He tilted his head in confusion.

"Oh, you're her," Silas said, chuckling.

"I'll get your brother." I pulled the large cotton shirt up to cover my exposed shoulder.

"Wait, don't go yet. I've heard a lot about you."

"Really?" It surprised me to learn that Ryker talked about me to his family. A warm feeling like a drink of whiskey heated my chest.

"To be honest, it wasn't all good, but I had a feeling there was something about you that stirred my brother enough to tell me about you." He turned his hat, and I saw the same brilliant blue eyes that Ryker had. They even held the same dimness caused by worry and grief. "I'm surprised my brother didn't chain himself to the door in protest when he found out someone had bought the old house."

I sat on the stool in front of the computer. "Oh, he did. Not the chains and all, but he tried his best to get me to leave."

Silas gave me a dimpled smile, and I saw the boy from the picture hiding behind the tough soldier. "He's had a real connection with it after what happened. Still blames himself, I guess."

"He told me about it."

Silas's eyes grew big. "He told you?" In all honesty, Mona was the one who'd filled in the blanks, but Ryker was the one who'd opened the door.

"Yes, we talked about it." Ryker's shirt kept falling from me, exposing my shoulder.

"What's your name?"

"I'm Ana Barrett."

"Well, Ana Barrett, no one in Fury has a real name. We'll have to figure out a nickname for you."

I'd never had a nickname, but it sounded like fun as long as it wasn't some stupid bird name like a booby or a smew. "People call him Hawk. What do they call you?"

He puffed up his chest and said, "They call me Rooster."

I nearly choked on my spit. "No way."

"True, but it fits. I'm up at the crack of dawn, and the ladies all want to lay my eggs." He gave me that disarming smile I'd come to expect from a Savage.

"I've got a friend who would love to meet you. She's got a thing for roosters."

He leaned forward, close enough to the screen that I could see his whiskers. "I'll look forward to showing her my c—"

"Rooster!" Ryker's bellow nearly knocked me off the stool. "Don't you dare talk dirty to my girl." He approached and put his hands softly on my shoulders.

I wasn't sure whether he'd be upset that I'd answered his Skype. "I answered it because I know you don't like to miss calls from your brother." There was a hint of fear in my voice. Ryker had a temper, and although I didn't think he'd hurt me, I also didn't want to find myself on the receiving end of his anger. It wasn't a pretty sight, and generally something had to be repaired once he was finished.

"I appreciate it." He pressed his lips to my cheek and kissed me right there in front of his brother. I don't know who was more shocked, Silas or me. Both of our mouths hung open like a door on one hinge.

I climbed off the stool and tried to walk away, but Ryker

wrapped his arm around my waist and pulled me close. He whispered low in my ear, "I came out of the shower, and you were gone. I didn't like that. Stay with me. I need you." He sat where I had been sitting and pulled me into his lap.

The whole time he talked to his brother, his hands were on me somewhere caressing my skin. He rubbed my arms. Drew circles on my bare thighs and nuzzled my neck a few times.

The brothers talked about the progress the investigator wasn't making; they had hit a roadblock again. The social worker who had placed their brother had passed away.

"Damn it, Hawk, maybe we need to find a new guy. The one we have isn't doing us any good, and he's charging us a small fortune."

Every muscle in Ryker's body tensed, and the surrounding air sizzled. I twisted in his lap and laid my head against his chest, hoping that a calming touch would extinguish the fire burning inside of him.

"I'm doing everything I can."

"You sell Dad's bike?" Silas's tone held a clip of accusation to it, as if Ryker was avoiding the sale.

"I've tried. There are no buyers. Some guy came out here yesterday and offered me two hundred bucks. I know you would have said yes, but I'm not selling that bike for the price of its gas tank. I'm not doing it."

Silas stared at his brother from the screen. "I wouldn't have done it either."

Ryker's muscles relaxed immediately. "I appreciate you saying that, bro. I'm doing what I can." His hand found its way under the T-shirt and splayed across my stomach. His callused fingers ran across my skin and sent a shiver down my spine. This man had a way with my body that made every nerve come alive with a touch. But it was the whisper of something more that sent my heart racing: "Go back to bed, I'll be right there. Be naked." The whisper was so light, I knew Silas didn't hear, but I was pretty positive he saw the red creep to my cheeks. My face was on fire, and it wasn't the only thing.

I slid off his lap. "I'm thirsty. It was nice meeting you, Silas. Are you coming home soon?"

Silas looked at his brother and then looked at me. "Yes, I think I might be."

I stopped at the refrigerator in search of something to quench my thirst and cool my heat. All I found was a six pack of beer and leftover pizza. I grabbed both and walked back to Ryker's room.

I pulled my phone from my purse and saw three texts from Grace. Knowing Ryker would be a few minutes longer with his brother, I dialed her.

"I'll be fine," she answered, as if she already knew what I was going to say.

"Are you sure? I could come home."

Grace let out a grumble, and I could imagine she was rolling her eyes. "Let me see…come home and sit with your pregnant friend or roll in the sheets with a hunky Savage. I don't know, Ana, which do you think I'd choose?"

"I remember a girl who sat on a lawn chair eating Chinese food and drinking decent wine out of Solo cups for me. I'll come home."

"Don't you dare. I finally got the couch to myself. Besides, the cable guy was here, and I've got a whole season of *Spartacus* to watch."

"We have a television and cable?" I couldn't believe it. I hadn't had cable in years, and the only television I ever watched was the glimpse or two I got in a waiting room or sports bar.

"Yep, all 189 channels. You could disappear for a month, and I wouldn't notice." That was a lie. Grace always knew where I was, and if I didn't answer a text or pick up a call, she was frantic. "Go bury yourself in the sheets and come up for air tomorrow. I've got it all covered."

Just then, Ryker walked into the room. Like the bird of prey he was named after, he swooped around me, moving the pizza and beer and tugging the T-shirt from my body.

"You were supposed to be naked," he said for my ears only.

"Gotta go, Grace. Ryker needs me." I hung up the phone without waiting for her reply.

"You got that right. I do need you." He looked down at the tent in his sweatpants. "It scares me how much I need you."

This time, his pace was slow. His seduction methodical. His skill unmatchable.

My body and soul were getting twisted with his in ways I never thought possible. When he entered me, he said, "I'm going to love you, Ana Barrett." Something told me that statement had nothing to do with sex.

Chapter 24

ANA

The next day while Grace was showing me her new bed, my phone rang. The number was one I didn't recognize.

"Hello?" I answered cautiously.

"Is this At Flight Graphics?" a female voice asked.

I couldn't say how long it had been since anyone called looking for my company. Grace was bouncing on her new mattress when I pointed to the receiver and mouthed the words, "Oh. My. God."

"Yes, this is Ana. What can I do for you?" I raced into the living room to grab a pencil and paper from my desk. The woman asked about logos and then asked whether I could design postcards and other promotional items.

"Yes," was my answer, and within minutes I had a new client.

Grace breezed past me and sat on the old sofa. "You're welcome," she said.

"What did you do?" I picked up my computer and held it to my chest.

She patted the cushion beside her. "I tinkered with your search engine optimization. I might have also tweaked your web page a bit. Then there was this hour that I posted to Facebook groups. And I may have sent it to my old client list. Other than that, I did nothing."

I sat down beside her and brought up my website. She had indeed changed things a bit. My new tagline was *Make Your Business Soar With At Flight Graphics*. It was perfect. In all honesty, she should have been doing my advertising. That was her specialty, but I never wanted to be an imposition.

"You are the best friend ever."

Grace smiled and tipped her head. "I know. Now tell me about your night."

I swept my tongue across my lips, thinking about the delicious way my body responded to Ryker's hands, his body, and his tongue. "Amazing. It was amazing. He is a complicated man, but I think there's more good in him than anything else."

"I'm glad." Grace's expression was warm and loving, but there was also a hint of longing that flashed past her green eyes. "I saw the way you talked about him, Ana. I saw the way he looked at you. I've never seen you connect with someone like that. I think you need each other."

"I think you're right."

I rubbed at the burning in my eyes. I'd spent another night in my contacts. "I need to take a shower and then get started on my new project." I slapped my hands and rubbed them together like a mad scientist. I had work. Real paying work that could turn into more.

While the water sluiced over my body, I thought about my new life. It was turning into something more, and that something more seemed good.

OVER THE NEXT SEVERAL WEEKS, I picked up a few jobs. I was growing a solid client base. I still hid birds in all of my designs, but that was part of the fun. Birds were part of my brand.

I was undercutting my competition, but I liked to eat, and work was work. Work was money. Work allowed me to get more done on the house. Work was security for both Ryker and me.

Nate was spending a lot of time with Grace, and that left me a lot more time to spend with Ryker. We slept mostly at my house because, in hindsight, he had already moved in before we started sleeping together. I wasn't sure that he'd even realized it as it was happening—I sure hadn't—but every piece of furniture he brought invested him into my life and home. And every gift I accepted brought him closer to me.

While I worked on my latest project, Ryker painted the exterior of the house light green. It was great to have a friend whose father owned a hardware store. When he asked me whether I wanted the expired paint, I didn't hesitate to say yes. Using expired paint wasn't the same as eating expired food, something I must have done recently with the way my stomach lurched today. Expired paint could make your house look better; expired food could turn your stomach.

The thought of throwing up brought the action on, and I raced to the bathroom with just enough time to lift the lid.

"You okay?" Grace stood in the doorway.

I rose from the floor and splashed water on my face. "Yes. I swear Hannah poisoned my food yesterday." My reflection in the mirror showed a pale face.

"You did swoop into town and steal her man." Grace crossed her arms over her chest. She'd been here for almost two months now. Her vacation and sick time were almost gone, and she'd have to make some hard decisions soon. In another few weeks, it would be hard to hide the bump that was starting to form.

"According to Ryker, he was never hers." I breezed past her and walked toward the kitchen. She followed. Mint tea sounded good right now, and it always settled an upset stomach. Maybe two pieces of pie last night hadn't been a good idea. Maybe mixing flavors had been an even worse idea. But I couldn't decide whether I wanted cherry or apple, so I got both and made a chapel pie. It had seemed like a brilliant idea at the time, but now I was rethinking my choice. "Tea?"

We moved together like a choreographed dance. I'd gotten used to having Grace here, and although I liked having time to myself or alone time with Ryker, I would miss her if she left. For a woman who initially made fun of Fury, she seemed to have acclimated fine.

"What's your plan?" I dipped and pulled my tea bag several times through the steaming water. Grams would be so disappointed. She'd been a firm believer in steeping tea for exactly three minutes, claiming it was the perfect time to avoid bitterness and yet pull the essence from the leaf. I, however, continued to dunk until my tea turned a translucent brown.

"Believe it or not, I have one." She rubbed her stomach with one hand and picked up her tea with the other. She followed me into the living room.

Without the pie in my stomach, I felt like a million bucks.

Grace curled up on the couch next to me with her computer in her lap. "I sent a message to the asshole."

I knew exactly who she meant when she said *asshole*: her boss, and the baby's father. "What did you say?"

"I told him that given my current ongoing condition, I thought a generous severance package would be the way to go. The man's a partner. He can make it happen." She looked over the rim of her cup. The steam rose to her flaming red bangs. "I might have also told him that failure to deal with the situation right away would require a paternity test."

"You're blackmailing him?"

Grace rolled her eyes. She'd been doing that since the first grade. Not even Sister Mary Mavis's ruler could break her of the habit.

"No, I'm asking him to do the right thing. I'm having a baby. I didn't get here by myself."

I sipped my tea and pondered the situation for a minute. "Do you want him in your baby's life? I mean, he told you to abort it. What kind of father would he be?"

She wrapped her hand protectively around her almost flat belly. "No, I don't, and if he wants out completely, that's fine, but he can't plant a seed in my womb and not pay to water it."

"Been talking to Mona, huh?" Those words were straight out of the Mona handbook for dealing with assholes. Mona didn't pretty anything up. She laid all the ugly out so it was clear. Grace and her mother, on the other hand, weren't close. It seemed obvious that Grace's mother had felt trapped in a hopeless marriage once she had a child. I certainly didn't want the same for my friend.

"I love that old lady. She's as ornery as a swatted-at hornet, but she's as sweet as simple syrup. And she does make the best lemonade on the planet."

I couldn't argue with that. Mona was keeping us supplied with lemonade. Grace drank it by the gallons, insisting that the vitamin C was good for her baby. I didn't have the heart to remind her that the sugar probably wasn't.

"So are you staying in Fury?"

There was no hesitation. "For now. This place feels like home to me."

I scooted closer to her and pulled her into my arms. "You're home to me, Grace, and I'm so happy that I might not have to give you up."

"Who are you giving up?" Ryker entered the house with splotches of light green paint all over him. The man looked good in everything and nothing.

I set my tea on the table and walked over to him. "Not you. I'm never giving you up." I rose up on my tiptoes and gave him a kiss.

"Good. I'm completely opposed to the idea of living without you." He gripped my ass and lifted me into his arms. "I'm ready for a break. What about you?"

That was Ryker's not-so-subtle hint that he wanted to rest between my legs, which didn't involve rest at all. I swore half the money I was paying him went to purchasing condoms. It was a good investment.

I rubbed at my itchy eyes and nodded. Despite their name, I was sure my extended-wear contacts weren't meant to stay in for days on end. However, I wasn't ready to let Ryker see the true color of my eyes. Most guys found them distracting to look at—freaky, even. Once, a guy had said it was like God couldn't choose between shit and sky. I'd even been told my eyes were the work of Satan. So now I kept them covered with simple brown lenses. It took the weirdness out of the mix. Complete heterochromia was what they called it, and only one percent of the population had it. I was one of the lucky one percent, and having it had made my adolescence a living hell.

While Ryker kissed me, Grace groaned, "Get a room," pretending to be annoyed, but I knew she wasn't. Grace wanted me to be happy, and Ryker did that. He made my heart feel full.

"We have one." He walked me down the hallway and kicked the bedroom door closed behind us. The loose floorboard tripped him, and he lunged forward, dropping me onto the bed.

"We have to add that to the honey-do list." I scooted back and looked at the man I'd grown to love. He was big and burly and often surly, but he was mine.

"I've got more important things to take care of right now." He pulled my pants from my body and dove into his next project.

Chapter 25

ANA

The next morning, while sipping my coffee, I looked out the front window across the street. Mona was standing on a step stool, trying to water the hanging plant on her porch. "That woman is a wonder and a menace."

Grace inched up to look at what I was seeing. "That woman is a saint. She's been good for me."

In all honesty, I thought she'd been good for everyone. "You know her last name is Charming, right?"

Grace let out a laugh. "Yep, it's kind of fitting in a weird way. Mona spreads her own brand of charm, doesn't she?"

Mona stepped down from the ladder and moved it toward the next plant before I left for the bathroom. I worried about her doing those types of things, but then again, she'd been taking care of herself long before I showed up.

The sound of Grace yelling cut my shower short: "Oh shit!" Her voice began to fade but not before she yelled, "Call 911!" I didn't even rinse off. I flew from the shower, pulling on my robe as I ran toward the living room, thinking that something was wrong with Grace or the baby, but she was gone.

My distance vision was shit, but even I could see Grace kneeling beside Mona. She was lying at the bottom of the porch stairs next to the fallen stepladder. I grabbed my phone and dialed 911 as I dashed across the street.

"Oh my God, Mona, are you okay?" I hovered over the old woman, who winced each time she tried to get up. "Stay down, the ambulance is coming."

"I'm not letting a fall keep me down." She tried to lift again, but I leaned over her, making sure she had nowhere to go.

My robe fell off my shoulder, and Mona gasped. Her eyes went wide. "Of course. That's why you have the house. It's yours. I heard rumors she'd survived."

I followed her line of sight to the scar on my left shoulder. "No, you've got it wrong. You're in shock. I got this from a car accident." I rubbed the puckered round scar that sat below the edge of my left collarbone.

The sirens got closer. Grace had gone to get a blanket and was back covering Mona up.

Mona pulled me down, so I was looking straight into her eyes. "I'm not wrong. You're her. You're Sparrow."

She was so certain, but I knew better. I knew who I was. I was Ana Barrett. My mother was Kathryn Barrett, and my father was Jayson Creed. They never married. They died in a car accident when I was four. *The same age as Sparrow.* The world dropped out from under me.

"Move aside," the paramedic said. I pulled my robe closed and stood back while he and his partner went to work. Mona was lifted to a gurney and placed inside the ambulance. I stared as it faded from view.

"Ana, are you listening to me?" I turned toward the voice. Grace's voice. Everything played in slow motion. Her hands were on my shoulders, shaking me. "Get dressed and meet me at the hospital."

While Grace ran ahead to get her keys, I moved like a sleepwalker across the street. Inside the house, she stopped me. "I know this is hard, but snap out of it. I know it feels similar to losing your grandmother. Mona will be all right, but she'll want us there."

I nodded as Grace, oblivious to the other reason for my shocked state, ran out the door.

I texted Ryker to let him know that Mona had fallen and was on her way to the hospital in Boulder. He'd left early in the morning to deliver his father's bike to a buyer in Denver. It was sad for him to see it go, but Ryker was like a protective pit bull when it came to his family. He was committed to finding Decker, and he'd sell his left nut if it would help. I hoped no one wanted that part of him, because I'd become attached to every part of him. Especially the lower half of him.

I rushed to put my contacts in and get dressed. The hospital was a good hour away, but if I hurried, I'd only be a few minutes behind Grace, and if Ryker left Denver right away, he might beat me there.

The whole trip, I thought about what Mona had said: "You're her. You're Sparrow." I couldn't be...or could I? A cold feeling swept up my spine. What if I was her? What if my entire life was a lie?

I'd never been driven by the need to research my parents' death. Grams had filled in all the blanks, but had she? Had she filled in the truth, or had she devised a tale to suit her needs? Why would she lie?

I pulled into the hospital parking lot fifty minutes later, grateful that Sheriff Stuart hadn't caught me speeding. Since I was a fan of Ryker, he'd decided he wasn't a fan of me. He'd already ticketed me for a broken taillight, and he'd pulled me over to check for my proof of insurance, all under the guise of making sure the citizens of Fury, Colorado, were following the rules.

When I entered the waiting room, Grace was there pacing back and forth. "She's in X-ray."

"Do they think she broke her hip?" That was my biggest fear. Older folks didn't recover from that type of thing. Generally, it went downhill after that. A tear slipped from my eye. I hadn't expected to gain a parental figure after losing Gramps and Grams, and now that I had, I wasn't ready to lose Mona. Although her guidance was flippant and often crude, she told it like it was, and I appreciated that.

Fifteen minutes later, Ryker walked in. His eyes were hard and his body tense. Seeing him this worked up made my heart rattle. He would be gutted if something happened to Mona. She was all he had besides Silas. He and I were in the same boat. We were orphans who had no one but each other and a few others. In fact, he had more than me. He had Nate and Mona and Silas, and hopefully, he could deliver Decker soon. I had Grace and Mona and Ryker, but how long would I have Ryker if what Mona had said was true?

I remembered his words verbatim from the day he talked to me about Sparrow. *I'm pretty sure if she was around today, I wouldn't like her much. I'd hate her for following me into the garage, and I'd blame her for everyone's death. The same way everyone has blamed me for years.*

Oh God. My stomach coiled and roiled. I looked in every direction for a sign that would point me to the bathroom. The blue sign blinked in the distance, and I took off running like a sprinter.

I hadn't put anything in my stomach this morning but coffee and stress. I never handled stress well.

I washed my face and pinched my cheeks. Until I had solid proof that I was or wasn't Sparrow, I refused to say anything. There was no reason to stab at Ryker's heart when nothing was concrete. I'd prove to myself that I wasn't her.

Ryker was leaning against the wall across from the bathroom door when I came out. "You okay?" He walked forward and wrapped his arms around me. I fell into his embrace. Everything inside me was right when he was around, and I knew I'd do anything to keep him—even if it meant keeping secrets. Hadn't I lost enough already?

"I don't do well in stressful situations." I leaned into his body as we walked back into the waiting room.

"I've seen you in stressful situations, and you're quite the spitfire." He teased me about standing up to him when most women would have folded and walked away.

I took deep breaths, trying to calm my pounding heart. He was right. I couldn't hide my fear behind the lie of not dealing with stress. But I couldn't tell him my real fear, so I said nothing.

Grace, Ryker, and I waited until a doctor came out to see us. He held out his hand to Ryker and nodded to me and Grace.

"Are you Mona's next of kin?" We all exchanged glances and then said yes in unison.

I wasn't sure whether Mona had family outside the strays she picked up in Fury. There was so much I didn't know about the old woman. And would I ever learn?

"No broken bones, but I have to ask why a seventy-two-year-old nearly blind woman is climbing a ladder." His eyes narrowed at each one of us.

It reminded me of the time someone had colored the nose pads of Sister Theresa's sunglasses with permanent ink. The bridge of her nose was navy blue for three days. I hadn't been responsible, but I'd watched it happen, which filled me with guilt.

"She is stubbornly independent," Ryker said.

The doctor shook his head. "That may be true, but you have a responsibility to make sure she gets help when she needs it."

He was right. We needed to take better care of Mona. I didn't push her off the ladder, but I'd known her climbing it was wrong, and I hadn't done anything about it. Guilt was wrapping its way around my chest like an invasive vine. It was squeezing my insides until I was sure I would suffocate.

As if Ryker sensed my tension, he let his fingers skim over my shoulders. His touch caused a war within me, and I didn't know why. I wanted his comfort, and yet Mona's words infused my brain with questions I couldn't answer. The most pressing was, *If I am Sparrow, can I ever be his?*

"Can she come home?" Grace asked. Her forehead was creased with worry. She'd really latched onto Mona, and I wasn't sure my bestie would be the same without the old woman pressing against her spine to make her stand tall and be bold.

The doctor shook his head. "I think we're going to keep her overnight to make certain the fall didn't jar anything else. You can go and see her. She's in room 112, but she's not happy." He looked down at his clipboard and walked off toward his next patient.

All three of us rushed toward Mona's room. She was already giving the nurse a hard time. "You call this lemonade?" She pushed the cup across her tray.

"I'll get you something else," the young woman said. She walked past us mumbling something like *that one's going to be a problem*.

"I'm not sure if I should hug you or turn over my knee and paddle you." Ryker leaned in and kissed her cheek.

"Don't tease an old woman. I hear that paddling is a thing these days and girls like it." She looked at me.

"Don't look at me. I'm not into that."

Grace stepped forward. "Sometimes it's good to be bad." She gave Mona a knowing smile, and I knew they'd be talking BDSM all night. Mona was old; she wasn't dead.

"Are you feeling okay?" I looked down at her bandaged ankle.

"It's a sprain, for goodness' sake. You'd think I broke my hip by the way you all are fussing over me."

I sat on the edge of her bed and held her hand. "It could have been so much worse."

She looked at me as if I was the only one in the room. "Some things are not what they seem. Often we get surprised to find out how things actually turned out."

I knew her words had nothing to do with her sprained ankle and everything to do with her speculation about my true identity. "Yes, things should always be checked out thoroughly before a diagnosis is made." She was a smart woman, and I knew she'd get my meaning. I didn't want her blurting out her suspicions. I wanted time to do some research. If I found out I was Sparrow, I feared my situation with Ryker would become terminal. That truth would be like fast-spreading cancer. It had the ability to consume both of us. I didn't want that.

I rose from her bed and looked at the two other people who were the center of my universe. "Since you both have it under control here, I'm going to drive to Denver. There's something I need to check out."

Grace smiled. "Finally going to get that new software?"

It wasn't my plan, but it was a good smokescreen for what I was about to do. "Yes. You caught me. Do you need anything?"

Grace put in her order for spaghetti and meatballs from Luigi's, and I was on my way. Ryker followed me out to the parking lot.

"Are you sure you're okay?" He cupped my face and looked at me with such love that my heart nearly burst.

"Yes, I'm good. It's just this whole situation with Mona is upsetting."

He brushed his lips against mine. "She'll be okay, but I better get back. Mona was plotting her escape when I left to catch up with you."

I laughed because it wouldn't surprise me to find out that Mona had broken out and gone home. "You better get back before she has Grace sneaking her out the back entrance. I'll bring dinner home."

When his lips descended on mine, all thoughts evaporated. It was Ryker and me, and nothing else mattered.

Chapter 26

RYKER

When I returned to Mona's room, she was tucked into bed with the blankets up to her neck.

"The doctor came in and gave her a shot for pain." Grace held Mona's weathered and frail hand in her own.

"I'm not sure if the shot was for pain or to incapacitate her so she can't get up and leave." Grace got up so I could sit down. "How many times do I have to tell you that I'll come over and help you? All you need to do is call."

Mona lifted her free hand to my face. "I saw her today." Her words were a bit slurred, and I knew the pain meds were kicking in. "She was there looking over me. She came to my rescue."

I knew she must have meant Grace or Ana, but something compelled me to ask, "Who?"

"Sparrow. She was there. You have to love her, Ryker. You have to forgive her. She's good for you." Mona's eyes fluttered and then closed. Grace and I looked at each other in confusion.

"It's the drugs," I said.

Since I assumed that Grace called 911, I knew Mona was talking about her, but she was confused. Grace was nothing like

Sparrow. Whereas Grace had bright red hair, Sparrow's hair had been brown. Grace's eyes were green, and Sparrow's had been unique. She'd gotten one brown eye from her mother and one blue eye from her dad. People used to tease her, and she would stomp her feet and then cry. It had been in those moments when I'd loved her the most. She hadn't gotten to choose her life. Her parents. Her hair color. Her eye color. Her death.

I leaned in and whispered in Mona's ear, "Sparrow is gone. She's never coming back."

I swore I heard Mona whisper, "You're wrong," but when I pulled back to look at her, she was sound asleep.

Turning to Grace, I said in a lowered voice, "I've got to run. Can you tell her I was here if she wakes up and doesn't remember?"

Grace followed me to the door. "She'll remember. You're not that forgettable." She continued with me all the way out to my car. "Tell me, Ryker. Are you in love with Ana?"

I leaned against my old blue Subaru sedan. "It's hard to say since I've never been in love, but what I feel for Ana is more than I've allowed myself to feel for anyone in years."

Grace eyed me with skepticism. "She deserves good things. Her life, like yours, has been marred by loss and pain, even if she can't remember it. Pain is etched into her soul." Grace stepped back. "Don't be her next source of misery. I'm begging you."

My head snapped back as if she'd punched my chin. I'd thought Grace liked me, but now I wasn't so sure. "I didn't go into this relationship with the intention of hurting her. In fact, I warned her away from me, but she's stubborn."

Her head nodded like one of those plastic dolls people stuck to their desktops. "That she is. She's also worth every ounce of patience and compassion and love you have to offer."

"I know that. I'm doing my best to be worthy of her. I'll do everything I can to be what she needs."

Grace turned to walk away but stopped mid-stride. "She said

you were a keeper. I think she's right. Are there more like you around?"

"You want to put two of me on this planet?" I opened my door and climbed in but waited for her reply before I shut it.

"You're right. One of you is plenty, but there's got to be someone for me. I can't go five more months being celibate."

"I've got a brother named Rooster. Maybe he can be your cock." I laughed my ass off at the play on words. It wasn't often that I was witty, and Nate always said my sense of humor had died with my parents. Maybe it was getting a rebirth after hanging out with Ana. She did bring out the best and the worst in me. Maybe someday I'd find a happy middle ground.

"No way is your brother named Rooster." Grace walked back toward the hospital, repeating that phrase.

"No damn way."

"No way."

"No…"

Her words faded in the breeze, and I shut my door.

Do I love Ana Barrett? I couldn't say yes, but I couldn't rule it out either. The thought of my life without her hollowed my heart, and now that it had been reconstituted from a dried-up, shriveled raisin-like pebble to a fully functioning organ again, I didn't want to live without her. I wasn't sure I *could* live without her.

Chapter 27

ANA

The minute I left the hospital, I called the Denver County Courthouse's vital records division. I gave the woman my name and birth date and asked if it was possible to search for my birth certificate, to which she replied, "Come on down and fill out the forms."

Surely, a birth record would prove I was who I'd always been: Ana Barrett, daughter of Kathryn Barrett and Jayson Creed.

An hour later, I stood in line, and when I got to the front, I took a big breath. "Can you please look for a birth record for Ana Barrett?"

Her wire-rimmed glasses sat on her nose. Her ponytail swung back and forth as she read from her computer screen. "I'm sorry, I don't have a record of birth for an Ana Barrett. I have a record of a legal name change to Ana Barrett that seems to match your time-line. Could that be you?"

I sucked in a breath. Could it be? I had always been so certain of who I was, but now I had this twisting in my stomach—a gut reaction from doubt. It was like I'd woken up to find someone had stolen my life. "I don't know."

I pinched the bridge of my nose and hoped the tears wouldn't fall, walking away from the counter. Something told me to run as fast and far away as I could, but I wasn't that girl. I'd survived whatever accident had killed my parents. I was a warrior, a fighter. I wouldn't back down.

Again, I stood in line, and when I got to the front, I whispered, "Can you look for the birth and death certificate for a Sparrow Creed or Sparrow Barrett?" I had no idea what her full name was, but if I were her, it would be one of the two. "Also, can you tell me if there is a death certificate on file for her parents?"

The woman tapped on the keyboard. "I must have the date of death." Her voice was robotic, like she asked the question a thousand times a day.

I rubbed the scar on my shoulder. I might not have had much memory of the accident or anything prior to it, but I'd never forget that date. "April 30, 1997."

"It will take me a bit to find them." The woman must have sensed my desperation, because her tone changed from professional monotone to a person who exuded warmth. "There's a coffee shop down the street. Go get yourself a drink. By the time you get back, I should have what you're looking for."

"Thank you," I said, but the only thing I wanted right now was to be Ana Barrett; however, somewhere in the knowing voice of my inner self, I knew she didn't exist. I was Sparrow. The girl who had ruined Ryker's life had shown up to destroy mine.

While I waited for my double shot latte, I did something I'd never done. I Googled my parents' names.

Halfway down the list of results was the article.

Massacre in Fury

April 30, 1997

Violence ripped through a small town in Colorado yesterday when two rival gangs went to war over the death of a motorcycle gang member of the War Birds.

Police have revealed few details of the latest incident, but a spokesman confirmed that former War Bird Darren Silver, also known as Goose, was shot dead when he pulled a weapon on Sheriff Sam Stuart during a routine traffic stop on April 14.

It is unclear what happened when Stuart walked into The Nest on April 30 to break up the mass gathering of gang members. The only witnesses were Lucy Warwick, 30, of Fury, who wouldn't comment on the events that led up to the massacre, Jack Johnson, 34, of Fury, who had no recollection of the events, and two unidentified minors, both children in critical condition. One is a four-year-old girl and the other an eight-year-old boy. The names of the minors are being withheld to protect their identities.

The deceased include:
Michael Savage
Michelle Savage
Sheriff Sam Stuart
Deputy Sheriff Eric Blunt
Jayson Creed
Kathryn Creed…

Although at least two-dozen additional people were listed, I stopped reading. My parents were married. I wasn't the offspring of a single mother and the man who didn't claim his child, like Grams had said. We'd been a family.

My stomach tightened into a knot, and bile rose in my throat. I swallowed it down when the barista called out *Ana*. That had been my name for over twenty years, but I wasn't truly her. I was a girl filled full of lies.

With coffee warming the chill that settled in my bones, I started for the courthouse. My feet moved across the sidewalk like I was walking through thickened syrup. I didn't need to go back for the records. I knew what they'd say. Jayson and Kathryn Creed had died on April 30, 1997. My birth certificate would say I was born on March 29, 1993—but not as Ana Barrett.

When I got back to the courthouse, the woman behind the counter held up an envelope, collected ten dollars and held my hand. "Your name doesn't define you. Only your soul can do that. Who are you, young lady?"

I hugged the envelope. "I'm not sure."

"Sweetheart, you're exactly who you were when you woke up this morning." She pointed to the envelope. "What's on those pages doesn't change a thing."

I gave her a weak nod and a weaker smile.

Outside, the sun shone. People strolled. Nobody noticed me, gave a shit, saw my secret. That's what it was. A secret. I couldn't tell Ryker my true identity.

On a bench in the middle of the park, I tore the top of the envelope free. I knew exactly what the birth certificate would say, but I needed to see it to truly believe it.

Four legal and binding documents said it all. The first two confirmed the death of my parents. The third, my birth as Sparrow Creed, born on March 29, 1993. The form slipped from my hands and fluttered in the breeze until I chased it down. I needed no more confirmation, but it was there in the last form that stated Agatha Barrett, the legal guardian of Sparrow Creed, had changed her name to Ana Lee Barrett on June 16, 1997. Less than two months after my parents had died.

My mind spun. I had lots of questions, few answers, and a message pinging my phone.

"Don't forget the meatballs, and bring two cannoli, and a half-dozen black and white cookies."

It felt like I took the first breath since leaving the hospital. Grace was going to gain a hundred pounds, come down with diabetes, or both. But Grace was here. She was my best friend. At least that part of my life wouldn't change. Nothing could take Grace from me.

I made a quick trip to Luigi's Italian Eatery before starting on the two-hour trek home. I thought about stopping in Boulder to see Mona, but what could I say? "You were right, Grams lied my entire life and will never have the chance to explain or apologize." I drove past the exit. Mona would be home soon, and maybe then she'd fill in more blanks.

When I got home, Ryker sat in the leather chair, reading a motorcycle magazine. He looked up and smiled. "Hey, babe."

Grace zoned in on the TV.

I breezed into the living room with a "Hi, y'all. I've got dinner." I tried to be the girl I'd been this morning, but even my voice sounded different.

I handed out to-go boxes, sat across from the doorframe with a plate of Luigi's pasta, and stared at the lines I'd refused to paint over. The lasting reminders I'd once been four and lived in this house. I'd run up and down the wooden floors. Bathed in the bathtub. Eaten in the kitchen and snuggled up to my parents in this living room. No wonder I knew where the bathroom was that first day when Mona asked.

I moved my meal around the plate, not eating much, and made an excuse to go to bed early.

"You look tired," Grace said. "Did you find the software?" She pulled a cannoli from the pink bakery box and licked at the filling.

Shit, the software. "It's an online subscription service. I'll download it tomorrow." I hoped that was true, because I didn't want to lie to her, too.

Ryker looked up from his magazine and moved the to-go box of spaghetti to his lap. "So it was a wasted trip?"

Grace sat up straight. "Wasted? Have you tasted a cannoli yet? This alone was worth the trip." She passed the pink box to Ryker, who opened it to look inside.

"I'll be in soon, babe."

I walked over and brushed Ryker's lips with a kiss. It broke my heart to think I would lose him if the truth came out. I couldn't lose him. I wasn't a liar, but I'd become one if it meant protecting him from more pain and protecting myself from a lifetime of loneliness. I deepened the kiss, hoping it wouldn't be my last.

"You stay up as long as you want. I'll be in bed when you get there."

He looked up at me with a deep furrow etched between his

brows. "I know you're worried about Mona, but she'll be fine. I promise it's all going to be okay."

I looked down into his soft blue eyes and gave him a weak smile. He didn't know everything had changed, and nothing would be okay.

After I brushed my teeth, I pulled on one of Ryker's T-shirts and climbed in bed. On the nightstand next to the lamp sat Grams' Bible. It had been sitting there since I'd unpacked her belongings. With shaky fingers, I picked it up and hugged it to my breasts. A tear slipped down my cheek and soaked into the gilded edges of the pages.

The woman who'd taught me everything was a liar, and now I wasn't sure whether I could recognize the truth in anything. I let the book fall open where it might. Sister Agatha always raised her old leather-bound Bible and said, "The truth lies in the pages."

I looked down to see where the book pages landed. Instead of finding the passage my heart sought, I found a picture and a letter in Grams' handwriting.

My dearest Ana Sparrow,

How many times have I started this letter and ended it? How many words have I written and erased? How many days have I sat in front of you drinking tea and felt the truth build on my lips but stayed silent? Too many times, and yet here I sit, again trying to come to terms with what I've done.

Let's start at the beginning. Your mother was a wild one. I see her in you. The way you stomp your feet and press your hands to your hips. That's your mother.

She graduated from high school and started college, and she met him. Yes, that would be your father. I didn't like him. He was older, wiser, and he had too much influence on my Kathryn.

I suppose that's what happens when you fall in love, and your mother fell hard. Jayson Creed was handsome, smart, and he took your mother away from me. She loved the bad boys. You have that in common with her. I can't say whether it's nature or nurture that molds a person since I raised you both.

Your mother left school and followed Jayson to Fury, Colorado. It hurt that she'd toss her life away on a man I didn't approve of, so I told her if she left, she'd be dead to me. I'll always regret those words.

Your mother had a huge heart and tried to mend our relationship, but I was stubborn. I stood my ground, and we could never fix what I had broken.

I looked around the room and tried to imagine a fight between Grams and my mom but couldn't because I never got to see that side of Grams. Regret and sorrow had turned her into the woman who raised me. She'd been present and loving, and she had listened to me. The only harsh words ever spoken had been about my dad.

Your parents married, and about a year later, you were born. She begged me to come meet you, but I wouldn't. Your grandfather visited several times. He came home with pictures of your happy life. I lived through his experiences.

Your father was a good man. He was college educated and smart. He ran his own graphics design company and specialized in motorcycle ads. So we come back to nature versus nurture, and I'd say you got your creativity from your father, so nature won out there.

But he was a member of a motorcycle gang called the War Birds. He wore leather, and jeans, and tattoos. I still don't like him, but it's not because he was a bad man. He was good to your mother and to you. It's because Kathryn chose him over me. Because that choice got her killed.

If she had only known my father wasn't responsible for mom's death. I was. If the stories were true, I'd knocked over the box, creating the sound that made itchy trigger fingers reach for their weapons, Grams should have hated me. I swiped at the tears flowing from my eyes.

I'll never stop blaming him for her death. I'll die blaming him, but I'll also die knowing I pushed my daughter away and lost five years of time with her.

Now back to you. Sparrow Annette Creed is your name. All the people in your circle adopted bird names. I thought it was silly. They called your mom, Finch. Your dad took the name Blue Jay. Imagine my surprise when you grew up obsessed with birds. Again, was it nature or nurture? I can't decide.

After the massacre, you came to live with me, and I was determined that you wouldn't be anything like your mother. When you had no memory of the shooting, I re-created history for you. I changed your name and raised you to believe your parents had died in a car accident. How could I tell you if not for a young boy named Ryker, you would be dead?

If the truth comes out, you should find that boy and tell him thanks. He saved you and saved me.

I'm sorry I lied to you. I'm sorry I sullied your father's name. I'm sorry I never got to tell my daughter I loved her one last time. The one thing I'm not sorry about is pouring everything that was good in me into you. I learned from your mother to love fully and openly because giving anything less than everything is a waste.

On a final note, I love you, Sparrow. You were the highlight of my life.

Love, Grams

My throat tightened, and I couldn't breathe. I swallowed the lump and buried my head in the pages. I'd opened the Bible seeking the truth, but I hadn't expected it to come from a letter addressed to a girl thought dead. I didn't know what to do with the confession I now held in my hands. Did I keep it buried in the Bible? What about Sparrow? Should she stay buried in the past? What about Ryker? He deserved to know the truth, but did I have the courage to tell him?

Chapter 28

RYKER

I woke wrapped around Ana's body. Her brown hair fanned across my chest. It was funny how life had come full circle. This was Sparrow's room. The same room where she'd insisted I play dolls. I'd refused until she let me bring GI Joe over to be Barbie's husband.

It had started out the same every time. She would insist that we get married, or at least our dolls would. I kept reminding her that my "doll" was an action figure, and he'd never do anything as sissy as get married. She always told me that I was wrong, and someday I would marry her.

In all honesty, I would have never married Sparrow—she was too strong-willed and stubborn—but even as an eight-year-old boy, I liked that she wanted me.

I rubbed Ana's back and wondered what kind of life Sparrow would have had if she'd survived to be Ana's age. Would she be married? Would she have children? The could-have-beens filled me with regret.

Mona was right; I had to let it go. I had to forgive myself. I had to forgive a four-year-old girl, who couldn't have known what would happen when she followed me into the garage.

I slipped from beneath Ana's body.

She didn't budge. Her breaths were long and even. Cocooned inside the comforter she slept. Ana Barrett was perfection, and I planned to let her know that every day of my life.

An hour later, I sat at the edge of Mona's bed. She was threatening mutiny if they didn't release her soon, but her doctor believed another day of observation would be wise. Not only had she sprained her ankle, but she'd also taken a good hit to the head.

"I had the weirdest dreams," she said. "Sparrow was holding my hand and talking about cannoli."

"That was Ana and Grace talking about cannoli, and they turned out to be amazing."

Mona sprang forward and grabbed her head. It was confirmation that another night in the hospital was wise. "You had cannoli and didn't bring me one? I taught you better."

"I didn't come empty-handed. I brought you this." I pulled a Snickers bar out of the breast pocket of my flannel shirt. It wasn't a cannoli, but it was what I had to offer. Mona had a sweet tooth, and I'd stopped at the vending machine on my way in. I held the candy bar out like an olive branch, hoping that she'd take it as a consolation prize.

Mona lifted her hand to my cheek. "You're a good one, Ryker. I don't care what anyone says." Gone was the strong woman I'd always visited, and in her place was a frail old woman I didn't recognize. This Mona had to get better, so the Mona I knew could go home.

"I thought everyone sang my praises."

"There are a few." She looked toward the door like she was hiding something, then tore the wrapper to the candy bar and took a bite.

"Snickers for breakfast?"

"I had to eat this. You were all out of cannoli." The ornery Mona I knew was back. "Where is Ana?"

I thought back to her lying on my chest this morning. How had I gotten to that point with her so fast? One moment I was telling everyone who would listen that I didn't do relationships, and the next I was spending every minute with the woman.

"I left her asleep in bed. She was exhausted."

"Youth…wasted on the young. If I woke up to a yummy thing like you in bed, I'd never be able to sleep. Show me those abs." She poked a finger into my stomach.

"You're such a cougar. How have you stayed single all these years?" Mona had been attractive when she was younger. Pictures hung in her house showed a pretty girl with light hair and big eyes. By the time we'd met, she was in her fifties but still attractive. I imagined if I were a geriatric man looking for love, she'd be at the top of my list.

"I always thought differently than most. My generation was all about getting married and having babies. I went into one of the few professions women could enter without getting looked down upon." She licked the melted chocolate off her fingers. "I guess you could call me a forward thinker. I wanted more than marriage and babies."

"Do you ever regret not marrying or having children?"

"Yes, and no."

I moved from the edge of the bed to the chair next to it. "Explain."

"I regret not having children, because it gets lonely and you're not around to tease all the time. I don't regret not getting married. It's not because I don't believe in marriage. I do, but I believe life should be savored, and I couldn't decide on one flavor. So I tried them all over and over again." She waggled her almost white brows. "Let's say that I refused to limit myself to one bite when I could enjoy a veritable buffet."

"Mona," I said with mock shock. "Were you a ho?"

"Do I need to ring the nurses' station and ask them to bring me a bar of soap to wash out your dirty mouth?" Her voice went straight to teacher mode, and that I'm-sending-you-to-the-principal's-office look crossed her face.

Leaning forward in my chair, I said, "No, do I need to ask the doctor to come in and give you a penicillin shot in case you contracted a venereal disease while you were tasting all the flavors?"

Mona curled in her lips between her teeth to stifle a laugh. "Call me uncharacteristically cool for an old broad. Now tell me about you and Ana. Is it serious?" Her look went from teasing and playful to thoughtful.

It was hard to define what Ana meant to me. "I'd say it's about as serious as a guy like me can get."

"You mean a wonderful, kind, and giving man like yourself?" She laid her hand over mine and squeezed. "Ryker, don't sell yourself short. You have so much to offer her. Open your heart and let her in."

"I have, and it terrifies me." I dropped my head, not wanting her to see the fear in my eyes. Loving Ana was the riskiest thing I could do in my life. She had the power to eviscerate me because she had filled my empty heart. What would happen if she vacated that space? Would it shrivel up and die again, and if so, would I die with it?

"Let love wash over you and fill you with its healing powers. Nothing can conquer love. Not hate. Not anger. Nothing."

I glommed onto those last words. Somewhere deep inside, I knew she was right, love was the only thing that mattered.

After another thirty minutes of chitchat, I told Mona that Nate and I had a lunch date and left.

When I arrived at the hardware store, Nate wasn't there, which was weird because Nate was always at work in the family business. I approached his father at the cash register and asked him where I could find his son.

"I sent him out to Bob Tucker's place to deliver the new

Redeeming Ryker

barbecue igniter switch Bob had ordered, but that was an hour ago. I'm getting worried."

"I'll take a ride out there and see what's got him hung up." Old man Tucker had about a thousand war stories in his eighty-year-old head waiting for a listener, and Nate was too nice to tell him no. I was near certain I'd find him on the porch, drinking cold coffee, listening to the old man tell him about the good old days.

When I turned onto County Road 19, my certainty tanked. Up ahead were the flashing lights of emergency vehicles. Lots of them.

The closer I got, the heavier my chest became. I'd seen enough flashing lights and ambulances to last a lifetime. It was when I saw Nate's motorcycle all smashed up and twisted around a tree that I panicked.

Lying on a gurney was my best friend. I raced to him, but the paramedics pushed me away. They were yelling out vital signs and pushing a needle into his arm. It was a bloody mess.

"Will he be okay?" The words choked out of me like a guttural cry.

"That's what happens when you drink and drive." Officer Stuart stood next to me chewing on a toothpick. "That boy surged past me, going way too fast. His bike was all over the road. I saw the whole thing. One minute he was on the bike, and the next wrapped around the tree."

The one thing I knew about Nate was that he'd never be drinking and driving. Hell, the man rarely drank, and if he had more than one, he always called a cab. This was no accident, and this son of a bitch had something to do with it.

"I hope he makes it," the sheriff said, but I wasn't sure the concern in his voice was genuine. "It would be such a tragedy for you to lose someone you care about."

I got his message. Junior blamed me for his father's death. He'd been waiting for years for payback. "You asshole." I gripped the sheriff's shoulders and pushed him backward. "You ran him off the road, didn't you?"

173

A sinister smile took over his ugly face, and I was certain he hated me enough to hurt Nate. "Boy, get your hands off me, or I'll take you in." He shrugged out of my grip. "Your energy is best spent praying for your friend and looking after that pretty little woman you have fooled. I hear accidents are contagious." The sheriff climbed inside his cruiser and turned off his emergency lights, as if his job was finished.

The wail of sirens split the air as I followed the ambulance to the hospital. The entire time, I hoped and prayed that Nate would survive.

Chapter 29

ANA

My mind was like Swiss cheese today. I couldn't put two sentences together to form a complete thought. I tried to work on my new project but quit when I put Jack and Kill Childcare instead of Jack and Jill Childcare.

Fixated on the information I learned, I had to decide whether to tell Ryker. Not telling him made me as guilty as Grams. Telling him could ruin everything. Ryker smiled more, laughed more, and lived more. To tell him would be to send him back to darkness and despair.

After hours of deliberation, I reached a verdict. I'd bury the truth deep inside me and never let it out. What he didn't know couldn't hurt him or me.

I picked up the photo of Grams and me. I couldn't have been more than seven, but I had no memory of the zoo, the aviary backdrop, the huge hawk cutout. But my smile cracking into a laugh proved me happy.

Maybe Grams had been right to keep the darkness from my life. I couldn't fault her for storing the truth inside her, or maybe that's what I was now telling myself to justify my lack of honesty. It was easy to tell a lie when you told yourself it was best for everyone, but wasn't that a lie, too? I was no longer certain of anything. I shut down my computer and tucked the picture under my keyboard.

My phone lit with a message from Ryker, and my heart took a hit. Nate in an accident, critical condition. His PLEASE COME all in caps.

I wasted no time in getting ready, and neither did Grace. She and Nate had become close friends, and the news of his accident hit her hard. She cried and prayed out loud the whole fifty minutes to the hospital.

In the waiting room, Ryker paced so fast, I was sure he'd wear a hole in the carpet. He looked tired and older. His eyes red-rimmed, he'd been crying or, at the least, holding back the tears. "Nate's in surgery. The doctors don't know if..." He rubbed his face with his hands. "He's hurt pretty bad."

"I'm so sorry." I pulled Ryker to a corner sitting area and tugged him down beside me. "What happened?"

Grace took a seat to his right. We both leaned in while Ryker described what he'd come upon. He fisted up and turned Heinz ketchup red when he mentioned the sheriff.

"Someone has to stop him." Ryker's yell was one part anguish, three parts rage, a volatile mix. He gripped the wooden arm of the chair, and I swear the wood gave under his grasp. I needed to get him out of here before he imploded.

"If he's in surgery, it will be hours. Come with me. You need to cool off. Grace will be here. Nate's parents are here. They'll call if anything changes." I gave Grace a pleading look, trying like hell to tell her to help me out.

"She's right. I've got this." Her eyes were puffy and red, but her voice stayed strong and convincing. "At least take a walk, or maybe a short ride."

I didn't give him a chance to say no. I led him to the parking lot. Once inside my Jeep, I took off toward a lake I'd seen on the way here. Ryker had mentioned that he liked to sit by the water when he was stressed. Now seemed like a good time to get him to his Zen place.

I PARKED at the end of a dirt road. "I can stay in the car if you want to be alone."

"I've been alone enough." He climbed out of the car and came around to open my door. "I don't want to be alone anymore."

Fingers twined, we walked by the lake, the water lapped against the rocky shore. Everything appeared calm when we knew it wasn't. It was a false feeling of tranquility, but an appreciated distraction, even if it only lasted for a moment.

Silence surrounded us for over fifteen minutes, and then Ryker told me something that ripped my heart to pieces.

"I could never understand why my life was so shitty," Ryker said. "Then you came around, and I realize now that I've been waiting for you. You are my truth and light." He covered my lips with his mouth and poured all of his emotions into the kiss. "It's like I've always known you without ever having met you."

I swallowed his sorrow, anger, despair, and stored them in my lying heart.

We sat on a rocky ledge and skipped rocks until the sun sat high in the sky. My omission weighed heavy in my chest, and I knew I wouldn't be able to look at him every day and keep the lie. I gathered my nerve to tell the truth.

His phone rang.

"He's out of surgery." The tension dropped from Ryker's stiff shoulders. "He'll be okay." He echoed Grace's words as if he needed to hear his own voice confirm the news. "We're on our way."

His whole demeanor changed. There was a bounce in his step and a smile on his face. This was the Ryker I loved, and there was no way I would cloud his good news with my horrible truth.

Chapter 30

RYKER

Ana sat at her desk and created art for a childcare center brochure while I thumbed through a Harley magazine for the third time. We had several hours before we could see Nate, and I was keyed up and fidgety. I'd already been over to Mona's, watering her plants and checking on the house. I wanted it to be perfect when she went home today.

Grace had left an hour ago to pick her up. I'd wanted to go, too, but those girls were too smart for my good. They knew I'd break the rules and sneak in to see Nate.

I stood and walked to the front of the window. Ana snapped her computer closed and came to stand in front of me "You're wound as tight as a spring. I'm going to take a shower. Find something to do besides wear a path in the hardwood floor." She tiptoed up and kissed me.

I paced a few more times and put my unspent energy to work. There were still a few items that needed repair, number one being the board I stubbed my toe on every night when I climbed into our bed. 'Our bed' had a nice ring.

With a hammer and nails, I tapped on the floorboards next to the bed. When I hit the end of one board, the entire thing lifted to reveal treasures I'd somehow forgotten. Sparrow was the first one to show me the old loose board and the special things she hid.

I lifted the plank and pulled out the items a four-year-old girl deemed important. A Barbie doll and a Highlights magazine. I laughed when I pulled out GI Joe's backpack and weapon stash. Sparrow had always hidden the items that made Joe an action figure instead of a doll. I slid my hand farther under the floor and pulled out a small tackle box.

It seemed weird going through someone's belongings, but I couldn't help myself. I flipped the latch and opened the lid. Inside was a trove of everything from baby shoes to pictures. She'd even saved the yarn and noodle necklace I made her for Christmas. I sprayed it gold, and she thought it was the prettiest thing in the world. Although in her words it sounded more like 'perdiest thing in the wold.'

I pulled everything out, one piece at a time. A movie ticket stub for Anastasia. She always told me she would be the 'pwincess.' I'd be her 'pwince.'

At the bottom of the box was a picture of a woman I recognized, but I couldn't place the face. I turned it over and written on the back was "Grandma A" in blue crayon. A kid's barely legible scribble.

Sadness clenched my heart because her potential died with her. I glanced at the picture again and shook my head. There was no telling why Grandma A looked familiar. I tossed everything back in the box and latched it shut. I considered putting it back under the floorboards and nailing it closed forever but didn't. This was all that was left of the girl who had filled my dreams and nightmares.

Instead, I hammered the floorboard in place and brought the box to Ana's desk. When I put it down, I knocked her keyboard to the floor, and a photo floated like a leaf on the wind to my boots.

My knees creaked when I kneeled to pick it up, and I almost fell over when I saw who was in it. Standing beside the woman I recognized as Grandma A was Sparrow, but she was not the four-year-old I'd lost in a firefight. This Sparrow was older. This Sparrow had survived.

I glanced around the room filled with birds. Fire raced through my veins. I knew. I stormed down the hall to the bathroom.

Ana's contacts and solution sat on the counter. Her clothes littered the floor. I wrenched back the curtain and looked into her startled eyes—one blue, one brown—and my heart carpet-bombed my chest cavity.

"How could you?" I grabbed a towel and tossed it at her. "You knew and said nothing. How could you?"

She scurried out, water dripped onto the yellowed floor, pooling at her feet. Her shaking hands gripped the towel. Her eyes flashed toward her contacts and grew wide. "I can explain."

"Get dressed now." I wasn't sure whether I should stay or go. One was dangerous for her, the other dangerous for me. I turned and stomped down the hall.

Her sobs echoed through the walls.

I covered my ears and screamed. How could she have done this to me? She was alive, and she'd never reached out. I paced tiny circles, waiting and waiting and waiting for her to dare to face me. For her to dish some half-assed excuse. For some reason.

Eventually, Sparrow entered the living room. Tears spilled down her cheeks. She opened her mouth to speak, but I held up my hand. I didn't want her excuses. I wanted the damn truth.

"Do you have any idea how thinking you died affected me? It ruined my life. How could you have not said anything?"

"I'm sorry." She collapsed to the floor, and I wanted to run to help her, but I couldn't. She'd been dead to me for years, and she'd be dead to me again.

"I just found out." She pleaded with her eyes. Those crazy eyes I'd loved as a kid. "I swear. Mona fell, and she saw my eyes, and she knew. I didn't want to believe it, but I found my name-change petition—"

"I don't want any more of your lies." I stepped back and looked out the window, where everything looked the same. But it wasn't. Everything had changed. Nothing would be the same. "That was two days ago, and you said nothing. Why?"

"Because——" She buried her head in her hands. "——I loved you——" Sobs racked her shoulders. "——too much to hurt you again."

I hurt too much to trust again. "Love me? You lied to me." The last time I was this angry, I'd pushed a man out of a second-story window and killed him. "You covered your eyes so I couldn't tell."

"I've covered my eyes since junior high school when I got teased so bad, I wanted to die." She crawled over to me and pressed her head against my legs. "I was going to tell you at the lake, but then the call came, and you were so happy. I couldn't take away that moment of peace you had, knowing Nate would be okay."

I peeled her from my body and watched her crumple to the floor. Somehow I still wanted to reach out and hold her, but she'd betrayed me. She'd taken what was left of my heart, brought it back to life, then squeezed it dry. I walked to the door with a calm I didn't feel.

"Should I call you Ana or Sparrow? Either way, the message is the same. Stay the hell away from me." I yanked the door open and looked back to her lying on the floor. "Never talk to me again," I said. "I'm going to keep believing you're dead."

I HAD no idea how I made it back to the hospital. Anger clouded my eyes, my heart. People say they see red when they're pissed off. I'd yelled so loud that the capillaries in my eyes burst, and I was truly seeing red when I glanced in the mirror.

When I walked into Nate's room, the bed was empty, and a sinking feeling settled in my stomach. The young nurse who had cared for him yesterday entered the barren space.

"They've taken him back to surgery. He's thrown a clot." Her eyes fell to the floor. "It doesn't look good."

The rage that had been geared toward Ana spiked to new heights. "When will the universe give me a damn break?" I snatched the pillow and threw it across the room. It hit the wall with such force that the hand sanitizer crashed to the floor.

The nurse backed out of the room. Her eyes searched for help. "I'm so sorry." She gave me a pleading look. "You can wait in the lounge. I'll keep you posted on his progress."

"You want me to wait so you can come tell me he's dead?" I rushed to the door and gripped the doorframe. "I'm not sitting around for more bad news." I'd had enough. I'd waited enough. I'd wished enough.

"People can't keep hurting me or the ones I love and have it mean nothing. Someone has to pay for this." I released my hold on the doorframe and threw myself into the hallway. "Sheriff Stuart, you stupid bastard, I'm coming for you."

Chapter 31

ANA

I rose from the floor and curled into a ball on the couch. I was wet and cold and scared. My phone sat in my palm while I pushed redial over and over. I pleaded with Ryker's voicemail to call me back, but he didn't. I texted him. My messages went unanswered.

Grace walked in the door, humming the theme song from Friends until she saw me curled in a fetal position on the couch.

"What the hell happened?" She cradled me in her lap. Her fingers brushed through my damp hair the way Grams' used to each time I cried. Grace had that mothering instinct, and I was happy to let her hone her skills on me.

In-between bouts of hysteria, I told her everything. Once I was finished, she sat in silence, as if digesting. Her hands stopped stroking my hair, and her breath halted. "Are you sure you're her?"

I rose from the comfort of her lap and went into the bedroom, where I'd hidden the envelope between the mattress and the box spring. One by one, I handed her the pages that showed my birth, my parents' death, my name change.

"It's all there in black and white and notarized."

"So, you're Sparrow." She walked to the kitchen and grabbed the box of wine and a glass. I gave her a confused look. "It's not for me, it's for you. If I weren't pregnant, I'd drown myself in alcohol with you."

She pushed the plastic spigot and poured me a glass. The rim had touched my lips when Grace's phone rang.

"It's the hospital." She pressed answer and pulled the phone to her ear. "He what? Oh, God."

I was so tired of hearing one-sided conversations. I gripped Grace's phone and pressed the speaker button.

"He's doing okay," the voice on the other end said. "He's stable. The clot was removed. There's no way to tell if there's permanent damage. It's wait and see. His parents asked us to call you. Do…" It sounded like the woman would say something else, but then silence filled the space.

"Hello," Grace said. "Was there anything else?"

The woman inhaled and exhaled. "I'm not sure if I should say anything, but Nate's friend was here. He left in a rage, screaming something about someone paying for this. Find him. He sounded deadly."

"Oh, God," I cried. "Ryker won't let this stand. He thinks it's the sheriff's fault. He will kill him, Grace. I have to stop him."

I grabbed my keys and ran for my Jeep. I had no idea where I'd find Ryker, but I would look in every corner and turn over every stone. Ryker might want me dead, but I wanted him alive and well. I loved him. I refused to let him ruin his life.

I went to the garage, the police station, and the diner. Initially, Hannah was caustic, but when I told her that Ryker was in trouble, her unrequited love sprang forth. She told me where the sheriff had a patch of land outside of town. On a napkin, she drew me a rough map, and I took off like a greyhound chasing a rabbit.

Each minute that passed was a minute too late. I pressed the gas and raced up the dirt road. My heart stammered when I saw Ryker's car.

I searched the area for him but came up empty. It was when I pulled past the house that I saw Ryker standing in front of the sheriff, who wore street clothes. His gun was nowhere in sight. At least that was something. No one was getting shot today.

But Ryker had a crowbar. Someone might get beat to death. I jerked to a stop in a cloud of dust that swelled around the men.

Ryker barely spared me a glance when I climbed out of the car. "There have been enough lies," he said to the sheriff, but the message was meant for me. I flinched at the anger in his voice.

"Admit that you went after Nate. Admit that you tried to kill him. Nate has done nothing to you, and he's lying in a hospital bed because you hate me."

The sheriff laughed. Odd, because this wasn't a laughing situation. His chuckle turned in to something more sinister, and the hairs stood up on my arms.

The sheriff took a menacing step forward. "You're right. I hate you. I've hated you since that day you lived and my father died. You ruined this town. You ruined so many lives, and now I get to ruin yours." Sheriff Stuart looked at me, then glared at Ryker. "You realize you're going to jail, right? You can't come on my property and threaten my life and get away with it."

My glance bounced between the two men. I wasn't sure who would act first, but anger and tension crackled around us.

Ryker raised the crowbar, ready to strike, and I turned toward him and screamed, "Stop while you can. Please don't throw your life away for this." I dropped to my knees. "Ryker, I'm so sorry. I should have told you the day I came back from Denver, but I was so afraid I'd lose you, and it happened anyway."

I twisted toward the sheriff. "Haven't we all lost enough? Haven't we paid enough?" The pain closed in on me; the weight crushed me.

The sheriff took another step forward, and Ryker pulled me off my knees. He pushed me behind him. "Don't you touch her." His voice was dark and deadly. He gripped the crowbar tight enough to turn his knuckles white.

Sheriff Stuart's jaw clenched. "You killed my parents." His eyes narrowed. "Now you threaten me?"

Threats. Lies. Fighting for nothing. Someone had to stop this insanity before another generation lost everything. I sidestepped Ryker. Only I could set them free. "He didn't kill your parents, I did." My confession hung in the silence. "I'm Sparrow Creed. I'm to blame." The minute I said my name, my world spun.

The sheriff's hand came up to scrub his bristly jaw. "You can't be her, she's dead."

"I'm not dead. I'm here." A jolt of consciousness zipped through my body, and I saw the past in living color. The scene from that day played out in front of me like a motion picture. Ryker as an eight-year-old boy. Leather jackets. Guns. Beer bottles. Old Sheriff Stuart. I pressed my mind for more. Flashes of memory came and went. My father and my mother. Ryker picking me up and tossing me. That's where it all slowed down. I was in the air for a second before I hit the box. A big man leaned against the tool chest. It fell to the floor, and I was in Ryker's arms while he ran to save our lives. The blow to my shoulder, the burning pain, and the blackness.

A strangled cry broke from my lips. "Oh, my God, I remember. I remember everything. It wasn't Ryker." I pressed my hand to my mouth. "It wasn't me. It was a big, fat man with a red R on his coat. The tool chest tumbled. The metal tools hit the cement floor. It sounded like gunfire."

Too tired, too lost, too alone, I fell to the dirt and cried for Sparrow, and Ana, and Ryker, and Silas, and baby Decker. I cried for Mona, and Sam Junior. For the dozen children who lost parents. The town of Fury, and for anyone affected by the tragedy. I cried until I was out of tears.

When I lifted my head, both men were on their haunches next to me.

"What the hell are you talking about?" Crowbar free, Ryker gripped my shoulders. "Tell me what you mean."

"It wasn't you, Ryker. It wasn't me." I looked toward the confused sheriff. "It wasn't him, Sheriff. You've been blaming the wrong man for years."

"I need facts." The sheriff crossed his arms. "Lay them out."

I swallowed the swelling sorrow stuck in my throat and explained how I'd followed Ryker into the garage. I didn't have many details, because I'd spent most of my time picking at a sticker on the box. "I saw my mom, and I made a dash toward her, but Ryker picked me up. I was facing the people in the garage when he tossed me toward the broken slat in the wall. Everything went to hell after that."

"If he had a big R on his coat, he was a Rebel." Ryker buried his head in his hands. His posture spoke of resignation and relief. "I wasn't responsible. I didn't kill everyone." He looked toward Sheriff Stuart. "I didn't do anything to get your dad killed."

The sheriff stepped back. His jaw twitched. His eyes moved back and forth like he was looking through files we couldn't see. His brain sorting through the evidence he'd most likely combed through a thousand times. "Tiny's the only man matching that description. They found him lying next to the tool chest riddled with fourteen bullets." A million emotions whirled across his expression and then stilled on realization. He'd been terrorizing a man who had suffered the same fate as him. It was when he looked down at both of us that a tear escaped his eye.

I nodded. I cried. I tried to be relieved the truth had saved Ryker. He was free, and no matter how heartbroken I was, I couldn't be sad for that. I couldn't lose him. "I wasn't withholding on purpose. I didn't know."

He rose to his feet and picked me up like I weighed nothing. "You can arrest me, Sheriff, but let me get my girl back to our home first. She's had a rough few days."

I pressed my nose to his chest. He called me his girl. I inhaled his scent. I was home. He was home. He was taking me to our home.

We almost made it to my Jeep before the sheriff called out. "Ryker."

"Yes, Sheriff?" Tense, he looked over his shoulder.

I clung to him, praying no more blows. That flashback and the emotions unleashed had drained me of the energy to stop them from destroying each other if that was what they were intent on doing.

"I didn't do anything to Nate. He was speeding and lost control. I used the situation to get under your skin. But I think it's time to bury the past, don't you?"

Ryker nodded, took me to the passenger side of the car, and set me inside. The buckle to my safety belt snapped into place, and he shut the door. My heart skipped a beat when he headed back toward Sam. Fear was a hard habit to break. I fumbled with the seatbelt, trying to get it loose in case I needed to intervene.

Sam picked up the crowbar Ryker had dropped and moved in.

My breath halted, and I watched the two men close the gap. But it wasn't in anger that they came together. Ryker offered the sheriff his hand. Sam looked down at it for a long second. These men had been enemies for a lifetime. Hatred was also a hard habit to break. But they shook hands, and Sam gave Ryker the crowbar. Ryker gave Sam his keys.

When he climbed into my Jeep and turned the key, the engine sputtered and died. It took three tries to get it to turn over.

"You need a tune-up."

I turned in my seat and looked at the man who, only hours ago, had told me he would pretend I was still dead. Now we were talking about tune-ups. "We're talking about cars?"

He put the Jeep into drive and then reached over to hold my hand. "You know you have a boyfriend who offered to work on your car."

I tilted my head in confusion. "You're my boyfriend?"

He stopped at the end of the property and turned toward me. "I am if you can ever forgive me for being such an idiot."

I wanted to make him squirm and tell him I'd think about it, but I didn't want to lie to him again. We were both to blame. "Can you forgive me?"

He leaned across the center console and wrapped his hand around the back of my neck. "I was angry and stupid. I'll spend the rest of my life proving to you that I'm worth another chance."

I unbuckled my belt and climbed over onto his lap. "I forgive you because I love you. I'm tired of hurting. I'm tired of seeing you hurting. Let's put the past behind us and look to the future." I pressed my lips to his and lost myself in the kiss.

He pulled away. "There's one more thing I need to know."

I leaned back and the steering wheel poked me. "What's that?"

"When I bury myself inside you tonight, what name do I call out?"

My laughter filled the air. "As long as you're buried inside my body, you can call out anything."

He cupped my chin, and his expression turned serious. "No, really, what do I call you? Who do you want to be?"

I thought about his question for a moment. "Sparrow was the girl you lost. Ana is the woman you found. I'm one and the same, but with you, I'd rather be the woman."

He lifted me from his lap and placed me back in the seat.

"Let's go home, Ana."

Chapter 32

RYKER

We went home and climbed into bed. The moment wasn't sexual. That could only come after I'd apologized at least a dozen more times. I'd been programmed to think the worst of people, to fight for everything, and it would take time to break those habits.

While Ana slept curled against my body, I counted my blessings instead of my curses. None of our lives had been easy, but we'd made it this far, and we would continue to move forward. Only this time would be different because the journey wouldn't be traveled alone.

Several hours later, we dressed and went to the hospital, where Grace and a recently discharged Mona sat in the waiting room. Nate had made it through his second surgery and looked like he'd make a full recovery.

When the nurse told us he was awake, I raced alone to his room.

"God, man, you did a number on yourself." He looked like shit, but his bruised skin was beautiful because Nate was alive, and it was good to be alive. "Do you remember what happened?"

He took a deep breath and winced. "Every damn minute of the

beginning. I was cruising at eighty with the wind in my face when I saw the sheriff up ahead." Nate leaned forward and tried to adjust his pillow.

I reached behind him and helped.

When he leaned back, he continued. "I tried to downshift, and the clutch got stuck. Next thing I knew, I was on the sheriff's ass. I whipped around him but hit the soft shoulder, and that was it. I remember seeing a tree race toward me, but that's all."

I didn't want to tire him out before the rest of the gang saw him, so I saved the story about Ana being Sparrow for later. Nate's eyes were already drooping, and I rushed out to shuffle the rest of the group inside before he fell asleep.

Ana and Grace raced ahead while Mona limped along.

"You were right, Mona. Ana is Sparrow." I slid my hand through Mona's arm and helped her shuffle forward.

She looked up at me. "Don't you know I'm always right?"

I laughed. "You're right again, you've never been wrong."

Softness settled in her hauntingly light eyes. "She's risen from the ashes. Don't let her get away."

"I won't." I cupped the face of the woman who had been there for me when no one else was around. "I love you, Mona."

"I love you, too, Ryker, but I still can't have your babies, so get that girl home and get on with it, will you?" She picked up her pace and limped into Nate's room.

It didn't take long for Nate to tire, and when his eyes drooped and closed, we all left. Grace went home with Mona to make sure she didn't need anything. That meant Ana and I would be alone for the night.

Back at the house, my car sat in the driveway with my keys tucked under the floor mat. It was the first of many olive branches I hoped to exchange with Sam.

Right away, I ran a bath for Ana and poured her a glass of wine. I'd done a lot of things with her, but I'd never romanced her. Wasn't it time? She soaked while I changed the sheets and lit candles in the bedroom.

When she emerged, I was waiting on the bed with the sheet pulled to my waist.

"You look like a sacrifice waiting to be claimed." She dropped her towel and walked her beautiful nakedness toward me.

"Will you claim me?"

She crawled like a cat from the end of the bed to my lap. "I will always claim you, Ryker. You've been mine since that day I gave you a daisy and asked you to marry me."

"You remember." It was one of my favorite memories, too.

I flipped her to her back and pressed my body on top of hers. Her skin was velvet smooth. She smelled so sweet. I traced my tongue from her neck to her core and swiped it along her heat. Ana was mine today, tomorrow, and forever.

I spent a lifetime between her thighs, making sure she was happy. She writhed and wriggled beneath my tongue, and when she tensed, I pulled away. "I'm going to make you scream my name, Ana, and when I do, I want you to call me Hawk."

Her smile lit up the room. Her body lifted as she sought more. I flattened my tongue and ran it through her sex until I reached the swollen button that would make her soar. When I pulled it past my lips, she took flight, and the name Hawk echoed through the quiet house. The heat of my tongue stroked every last quiver from her body, and when she lay sated and happy, I climbed between her legs and claimed her as mine forever.

Stroke after stroke, I promised myself to this woman who had risen from the dead to bring me life. When the beginnings of my climax tightened my stomach, I stilled inside her and said, "You are my Phoenix, and I'll love you until my dying breath," before emptying myself in her. All of me. I gave her my mind, my soul, and my body, but most importantly, I gave her my full beating heart.

Chapter 33

ANA - TWO MONTHS LATER

I was putting the finishing touches on a painting of—what else—a bird when Grace burst through the door, waving a black and white picture through the air.

My palette hit the desk, and I ran to her side. On the glossy photo, an arrow pointed to a tiny penis, and the words "it's a boy" were typed above.

We both laughed and jumped up and down until our bellies ached. "I'm so excited. I will be an aunt." We weren't a traditional family. None of us were connected by birth, but we were a family, nonetheless. A strong family because we were connected by choice.

Grace looked at my latest painting. I'd brought over the pictures from Hawk's place and hung them in a row on the wall. Above every frame, I'd painted a picture of the bird the person was nicknamed after. The living room was like an aviary with art that spanned the range from a finch to a rooster to a parakeet. That was Grace, because she was tiny and colorful, and full of surprises.

"Leave a space for my little man." She rubbed her hand over her growing tummy. "I'm thinking this might be a good place to raise him." She grinned.

"You're staying?"

"You couldn't drag me away." Grace no longer lived with me, but she hadn't gone far. With money from her severance package, she rented a house down the street and divided her days between Mona and me. Mona refused to be named after a bird. Behind her back I called her Hen, because she clucked around all of us like a mother, protecting her chicks.

Grace headed to the door. "I've got to go. Nate's sitting with Mona, and I'm sure he needs saving. Besides, Mona is waiting to find out what we're having."

"You're sounding like a couple."

Grace laughed. "Pathetic, I know, but until you find me a rooster who won't mind hatching another man's egg, she's all I've got."

I knew a rooster who might be up to the task if we could ever get him to leave the desert and come home. But for now, I kept my mouth shut.

Grace walked across the street, and I thought about how amazing my life had turned out. I'd left the name Sparrow behind and adopted the name Phoenix—a mythical bird that rose from the ashes to live a new life. A life full of love, and hope, and promise.

Hawk walked in with a paper bag from the grocer's and a box from the diner. I'd had a thing for chocolate cake lately. It was an insatiable craving that couldn't be satisfied. I pulled the grocer's bag from his hands and went to the bathroom. If we were right, Grace wouldn't be the only one having a baby.

Five minutes was a long time to wait when you knew the results of a test could change your life. When I walked out, Hawk was Skyping with his brother. He was telling him that the investigator had turned up another lead. They seemed to get closer to finding Decker, and with each new lead, I watched the brothers change. Doubt had been replaced with optimism.

I stood behind my man so Rooster could see me as well. "I took the pregnancy test." I kept my face neutral, so I gave nothing away.

"What's it say?" Ryker turned toward me. Both men went silent and waited. I waved the stick around in the air the same way Grace had waved her ultrasound picture. He grabbed my wrist and pulled the test toward him. Crisp clear letters that spelled the word pregnant showed in the window.

"I was thinking, boy or girl, how do you like the name Wren?"

He pulled me onto his lap and kissed me. We had all but forgotten Rooster was still there until he said, "If I'm going to be an uncle, I should come home. My niece or nephew will need the influence of a hawk and a cock to survive Fury."

I'd never seen Ryker so happy. All of his dreams were coming true. He had a home and a family, and one of his brothers was coming back to the nest. I thought about Grace and smiled. Life had a way of giving you what you asked for. She'd asked for a rooster, and he was on his way.

NEXT UP IS *Saving Silas*

Other Books by Kelly Collins

The Boys of Fury Series

Redeeming Ryker

Saving Silas

Delivering Decker

The Boys of Fury Boxset

Wilde Love Series

Betting On Him

Betting On Her

Betting On Us

A Wilde Love Collection

About the Author

International bestselling author of more than thirty novels, Kelly Collins writes with the intention of keeping love alive. Always a romantic, she blends real-life events with her vivid imagination to create characters and stories that lovers of contemporary romance, new adult, and romantic suspense will return to again and again.

For More Information
www.authorkellycollins.com
kelly@authorkellycollins.com

Acknowledgments

First and foremost, I want to say that I have the most amazing husband and children. Without their support, a word would never get written. They are my reason for everything.

Redeeming Ryker became a thought in early 2016 when I woke up and said, "What if everything you thought you knew about yourself was a lie?" That "what if" turned into a book, which will be a series.

As a writer, I find the words, but they are never as pretty as they can be. That's where the skill of an editor comes in handy. I want to thank Sadye and Karen Boston for their hard work on this book. This story has special meaning to me.

A big thanks to Tammy and Tiffany for proofreading because no matter how many eyes see the pages something is always missed.

Rhay, your critiques were spot on.

Now, to you, the reader. I spend my life buried in words because you love to read them. Thank you for your support, for your words of encouragement, for writing and telling me what you thought. It's for you that I sit in my office and spin stories. Without you, there wouldn't be a reason.

Hugs,
Kelly

Printed in Great Britain
by Amazon